The Christmas Heist:

A Courtroom Adventure

To Jane,
Always Believe!

The Christmas Heist: A Courtroom Adventure

Trade 978-0-9861516-5-1
eBook 978-0-9681516-6-8

Library of Congress Control Number: 2015947965
Fiction-Fantasy General

Cover and interior illustrations by
Susanne Discenza Frueh, sfrueh@gmail.com

Book Design by Frogtown Bookmaker,
www.frogtownbookmaker.com

Published by Lystra Books & Literary Services, LLC
391 Lystra Estates Drive, Chapel Hill, NC 27517
919-968-7877
www.lystrabooks@gmail.com

Printed in the United States of America

LYSTRA BOOKS
& Literary Services

Praise for *The Christmas Heist*

Lawyers and tax collectors, can there be any more hard hearted people on the planet? Yet, this lovely Christmas tale by Landis Wade may restore your faith in a humanity that believes and cares. A modern day court battle pits wrong against right with Christmas in the balance. And how do they keep that "naughty and nice" list? I will never pass by a Salvation Army bell ringer again without wondering if they have some Christmas secret to tell. Be sure to add this story to your Christmas traditions.

Major Larry Broome,
Area Commander, The Salvation Army

The Christmas Heist: A Courtroom Adventure brings the magic of *Miracle on 34th Street* into the modern day. The twists and turns of this courtroom drama surprise and delight and have the reader believing all over again!

J.D. DuPuy
author of *Poetic Justice, Legal Humor in Verse*

Give yourself a present this Christmas. Forget Rudolph reruns and skip the DVD of *It's a Wonderful Life*. Renew your spirit instead with this laughable, lawyerly look at the case of Santa Claus vs. the internet. It's a win-win.

Mary Ann Claud, author of *The Dancin' Man*
and *Whirlygig: The Dancin' Man's Daughter*
(coming spring, 2016)

Even our favorite North Pole resident and his helpers have gone digital and they're not immune to glitches. When it all ends up in a courtroom two days before Christmas, we're into a fine holiday tale. Landis Wade gives us a fast-paced story in the lineage of *Miracle on 34th Street* and the Grinch, fun to read and just right for the season. Sit back, pour the eggnog, and enjoy.

Joyce Allen,
author of *Hannah's House* and the *Threads* trilogy

Anyone who has spent any time in the justice system will recognize the courtroom and its players in Landis Wade's opening scene. The judge, prosecuting attorney, defense counsel, defendant, and prosecuting witness live in Anywhere, USA–until the witnesses transport us to unfamiliar places where we are very willing to go. Landis Wade writes a script somewhere between the screenplays for *My Cousin Vinny* and *Miracle on 34th Street*, and that's a wonderful place to be.

Suzanne Reynolds, Dean,
Wake Forest University School of Law

I found this book creative. Mysterious. Imaginative. Funny. Fun. The descriptions of people and places are so vivid that it feels like I'm there with the characters. And the story is told in a magical way. When I let my imagination loose, I was flooded with memories of Christmas.

Jeffrey J. Davis, author of *Beliefs and Choices*

To Mom and Dad, for the Christmas excitement
you gave me as a child;

To Jordan and Hamlin, for the joy of Christmas
when you were children;

And to my wife Janet, for always keeping
Christmas in your heart for a Scrooge like me.

THE CHRISTMAS HEIST:

A Courtroom Adventure

by

Landis Wade

LYSTRA BOOKS
& Literary Services

Chapel Hill, NC

Really, for a man who had been out of practice for so many years, it was a splendid laugh, a most illustrious laugh. The father of a long, long line of brilliant laughs!

Charles Dickens, *A Christmas Carol*

10:30 a.m.

The county courthouse was opening for business two hours late. Early morning sleet and ice were the cause of the delay, but the streets were improving and the halls of justice were just beginning to heat up. For many who graced the halls that Monday morning, it was a bad place to spend a December day, but to optimists, and those who had faith, it was tolerable, because it was one day closer to Christmas than the day before.

People of all shapes, sizes and colors were in the security line at the front entrance, and the metal detectors were ringing, but the sound was not in synch with the tune of the pending holiday. Instead, it was the sound of clanging shiny things like loose change, pens, keys and every now and then a knife that some unfortunate entrant forgot was in his back pocket.

A large white man wearing a red flannel shirt shuffled along as the line moved forward. He was Henry Edmonds. He must have been close to 6 feet 6 inches tall, and likely tipped the scales at around 275 pounds. His face, covered with salt-and-pepper stubble, was interesting, but his eyes were sad, downcast. His age was indeterminate, but not less than sixty-five years.

When he pulled his tight wool cap off at the conveyor belt, white hair fell loose, down to his shoulders. He stuffed his hat in his Carhartt work coat and shed the coat for the conveyor belt that passed through the weapon detector under the watchful eyes of a sheriff's deputy. The only other thing in his coat pocket was the key to the 20-year-old Ford pickup truck he had driven to the courthouse that morning. He had nothing else with him because his lawyer made it clear he needed to travel light, and bring nothing but himself to court.

Judy Robertson was also in that line, ten people back from Mr. Edmonds. She wore black shoes with two-inch square heels, and a black knee-length coat that covered a gray pinstriped pantsuit. Her hat sat atop auburn hair clipped close to her neck and ears. Her eyes were firmly fixed on the large man with the white hair.

This day had a purpose for the woman. She needed something and she planned to get it. Henry Edmonds would not get in her way. In fact, he was the reason she was here. According to the official record, she was the victim, and he was the perpetrator. They were both headed to the same place, a criminal courtroom on the third floor.

11:00 a.m.

Thirty minutes later, in that third-floor courtroom, a bailiff stood quickly, dropping his magazine in the process. He looked to be about 5 feet 4 inches in all directions, but what he lacked in physical fitness, he made up for with his acute sense of timing. Just as he stood, a door to his left opened and a tall figure in a black robe emerged.

"All rise!" the bailiff bellowed, with as much bellow as his round frame could muster.

Everyone in sight did just that. And then they listened carefully for the next set of instructions.

"Oyez, oyez, oyez, this honorable court of this great State is now in session, the honorable Augustus Langhorne Stark, judge, presiding. Be seated and come to order!"

And with that, the judge walked purposely up the three steps to the bench he would call home for the next few days. And he sat down.

Judge Stark had a stoic expression on his face. His pursed lips and drawn features did not convey kindness, nor anger, but rather, a seriousness of purpose that had become his calling card. Some in the courtroom who saw him take his seat on the bench that morning thought he looked indifferent, while others thought he was about to strike a legal blow at somebody. Others could not be sure. But one thing was for certain: Neither Judge Stark, nor his serious look, went unnoticed by the attorneys and their clients who were waiting to appear before him.

Judge Stark usually presided over felony criminal cases and large-dollar civil disputes, but the legislators in the capital city, believing they understood better than the judiciary how to run the court system, had decided that judges should be required to hear all kinds of cases, including misdemeanor criminal matters. This was just one of the many reasons Judge Stark was planning to retire.

Judge Stark's rotation for the week placed him in criminal misdemeanor Courtroom 3150, the courtroom he liked least of all. He had a reputation of being a person who wanted things to run smoothly, a man of order, a man of structure and a man who believed that people should be on time and get to the point. Truth be told, this was the one courtroom where his hoped-for order, structure and getting to the point tended to be the exception, not the rule.

Courtroom 3150 went by the nickname "the People's Court," because it was regularly flooded with regular people committing regular crimes and getting regularly convicted. On the other hand, there was nothing regularly truthful about the stories told in the People's Court. The defendants, often short on education, were long on creativity when it came to telling their stories. Alibis were like poetry. Defenses like good prose. Only, on this day, Judge Stark would write the endings of each little tale.

Getting right to work, the first case he ordered for trial was captioned: The State v. Henry Edmonds.

Jason Peabody was the assistant district attorney on the case against Mr. Edmonds. If it was unusual to find Judge Stark in Courtroom 3150, it was equally strange to see Peabody there. Peabody had ten years of experience as a prosecutor and was good at his craft. On any given day in the People's Court, one would find a younger, less experienced prosecutor representing the interests of the State. The fact that Peabody was here and not trying a felony case in another courtroom was a small mystery.

In the People's Court, there is no jury. When you lose your case in Courtroom 3150, you can appeal and get your jury trial. But in this court, and on this day, Mr. Edmonds' fate was in the legal hands of the not-so-friendly-looking man on the bench.

"Mr. Peabody," Judge Stark said, "I understand this is a case charging assault and petty larceny of some kind, is that right?"

"Yes, your honor. Mr. Edmonds is charged, in the first count, with assault, to wit: pushing the victim to the ground and causing her pain and suffering; and in the second count, larceny, to wit: stealing a flash drive from the victim. Mr. Edmonds has pleaded not guilty. The State plans to prove his guilt beyond a reasonable doubt."

Judge Stark seemed bored already. "Call your first witness, Mr. Peabody."

The first witness for the State was a white woman in her mid-twenties, not unattractive, but a bit unkempt and tired looking. She was thin and wore her long straight brown hair parted in the middle. She wore blue jeans, work boots and a sweatshirt with a high-school logo.

After being sworn in by the bailiff, she turned in her seat to face the assistant district attorney.

"Ma'am," Peabody said, "please state your name for the record."

"Shelley," she answered.

Judge Stark, who had been looking down at some papers on the bench, and wondering how long this case was going to last, raised his head and eyebrows to look in the direction of the woman.

"Your full name, please," Peabody said, aware of the watchful eyes of Judge Stark.

"Shelley Barker," she responded, without realizing her infraction.

"Now, Ms. Barker, where were you on the night of November 20th of this year?"

"I was minding my own business, that's for sure."

"Of course you were," Peabody said, looking down for a moment and trying to act composed. Looking up again, and looking directly at his witness, he asked Miss Congeniality if she could tell the Court exactly where she was that night.

"I told you before you had a deputy drag me down here today, I was over at the Tipsy Tavern, on 9th Street."

"We certainly do appreciate your cooperation, Ms. Barker," Peabody said, trying as hard as he could not to let the sarcasm he felt creep into his tone. "But it would certainly aid the Court if you could tell us what you were doing at the Tipsy Tavern on 9th Street."

"I wasn't drunk, if that is what you're trying to find out."

Judge Stark looked at Peabody as if to ask, where did you find such a bright and stellar lead-off witness? Peabody quickly continued.

"I wasn't trying to find out anything, Ms. Barker, other than why you were at the Tipsy Tavern."

"If you must know," she said, "I went there to have one drink," with her emphasis on the word "one."

"So, did you have more than one drink, Ms. Barker?" asked the assistant district attorney.

"I certainly did not," she said with emphasis, as if to make it abundantly clear that she was an honest person.

At that, Judge Stark looked at his watch, leaned back in his black leather chair and sighed. Every witness who appeared in his courtroom, particularly the defendants, had the superb willpower to stop consuming alcohol after one drink. The sheer coincidence of this fact, which showed up in practically all Judge Stark's criminal cases, was not lost on him. Today, it was just one drink at the Tipsy Tavern.

Peabody pressed on. "And was the tavern crowded that night?"

"It was a pretty good crowd." She looked straight at him, pleased with her direct response, except that it was too direct. Peabody simply looked at her, as if to say: "What else, you idiot?" And she took the hint.

"There were a few people at the bar, half a dozen on the dance floor and a handful around the pool table," she explained.

"And what time were you there?"

She began to wonder if court was always this slow. She decided to tell it her way and get the thing over with. "I got there at around 7:30, and I stayed until that woman over there," pointing with her right forefinger to Ms. Robertson, "starting shouting and carrying on like her pants were on fire, and then—"

"Objection," the lawyer at the other table said, in matter-of-fact tone.

He was the defense lawyer, Thad Raker, a well-respected young lawyer with a solo law practice. Raker had been practicing almost as long as Peabody, which made the significance of their presence in this case even more curious. The defendants in this courtroom were usually represented by the public defender.

When Raker objected, Ms. Barker looked at him, contempt written on her face, but before she could tell him how rude it had been to interrupt her, she heard a deep, firm voice to her left say, "Sustained."

She turned to take on her new adversary, but was jolted back to reality when she found herself looking directly into the unfriendly eyes of Judge Augustus Langhorne Stark.

The courtroom got quiet.

"Ms. Barker, is it?" Judge Stark asked.

"Yes," she said, more like a question than an answer.

"Let me explain to you how this is going to work today. The man over there is the assistant district attorney. He is going to ask you questions. Your job is to answer the questions he asks. You may recall that he asked you a question about the time you were at the tavern. He did not ask you what you saw, or when you saw it, or whose pants were on fire. I suspect he will ask you about that in a moment. But in the meantime, pay attention to his questions and answer those questions and only those questions. The man over there, who made the objection, has a job to do, and his job is to object if he thinks you don't follow this rule, and it is my job if he does object, and that objection is appropriate, to make sure you behave. If I say 'sustained,' you need to pay close attention, because that means you didn't follow the rules. Are we clear?" he asked.

Ms. Barker looked at him in disbelief, probably thinking to herself: What kind of crazy rules of law do we have in this country? If I say too little, the DA treats me like a moron, and if I say too much, the judge "sustains" me. No wonder the criminals go free.

But looking at Judge Stark, she just nodded in response, having the good sense to keep her thoughts to herself. She turned back toward Peabody, and said, "I came at around 7:30 that night and left around 9:00."

"Ms. Barker," Peabody said, "please take a look at the defendant seated at the table to my right. He is wearing a red flannel shirt, and he is sitting next to his lawyer who is wearing a brown suit. Have you ever seen him before?"

"Which one, the lawyer or the defendant?" she asked.

Judge Stark's chair creaked as it made a turning motion toward the witness, which she heard just in time to correct herself.

"I never saw the man in the brown suit," she said, "but I have seen the other man, the defendant, just once, on that night at the Tipsy Tavern."

"On November 20th?"

"Yes."

Before the next question was asked, the main door to the courtroom opened and a man entered. To those who saw him, he stood out, because he was the shortest man in the room, not more than 3 feet tall. Though small in stature, he had good posture and held his head high. His black suit was well-tailored and his shoes shone bright. His tie had a firm knot and the design on the tie fit the holiday season, small green trees on a red background. After coming through the door, he stopped in the aisle separating the two sides of the courtroom and looked around. Edmonds sensed the little man before he saw him and turned to face the door. The two found each other and locked eyes. After a moment, the little man took a seat in a pew on defendant's side of the courtroom. He opened the briefcase he was carrying, took out a computer and blended into the proceeding.

Assistant District Attorney Peabody paused to look at his notes, thinking about where to go next with the iffy Ms. Barker, when Judge Stark interrupted his thoughts.

"Mr. Peabody," interjected Judge Stark, "it is December 23rd, and if we are to finish this short trial in time for Christmas, we need to move it along. Understood?"

Peabody, being duly prodded, got right back to work. "Ms. Barker, would you tell the Court what the defendant was doing when you first saw him that night?"

"He was sitting at the bar."

"And how long were you at the tavern after you first saw him?"

"Long enough to see the fireworks—" She corrected herself, "I mean, I was there for about an hour after I first saw him."

"Did you speak with him?"

"No."

"What made you notice him?"

"Don't know for sure," she said. "I guess it was because he was in a tavern, sitting at the bar drinking milk, and also because he seemed out of place."

"How do you mean?"

Rather than answer the question, she said, "I didn't even know they kept milk in a bar."

Judge Stark's chair squeaked as it turned toward the witness and Barker quickly got back on track.

"Anyway," she said, "he wasn't a regular, and he was a little old for the usual crowd. He just sat there. Drinking his milk."

Peabody pressed on. "Ms. Barker, please tell us whether you observed anything happen that night involving the defendant."

She thought, finally, I can tell the judge what happened and get out of here. So she began.

"Everything started shortly after that woman," pointing to Judy Robertson, "walked in the front door, went to the bar, and took a seat beside that man," pointing again, this time to Henry Edmonds.

"Why did you take notice of them sitting together?" Peabody asked.

"Because she was way out of his league. He was old, wearing jeans and a flannel shirt, the same red shirt he has on today, and she looked like she belonged on the cover of some magazine for fancy women's clothes."

"What happened next?" Peabody asked.

"They were talking to each other, and I heard her say in a loud voice—"

"Objection, hearsay," Raker said.

"Dang right, it was hearsay," she said, "I heard it all the way from the other end of the bar."

As the gavel slammed onto Judge Stark's bench, just a few feet from where the witness was sitting, she realized her mistake.

"Ms. Barker." Judge Stark held the gavel like a hammer and pointed it toward her. "Have you ever heard the phrase 'contempt of court'?" Without pausing for an answer, he continued. "First, there will be no swearing in my courtroom, and second, you will not criticize the lawyers. That is my job, not yours. If you behave this way again, you will need a toothbrush, because you will be spending the night in one of our fine publicly owned facilities known as a jail. Is that how you would like to spend your Christmas?"

She shook her head in the negative.

"Well, then, I suggest you take my advice."

She nodded in the affirmative and kept quiet.

"Good." Judge Stark then turned to face the lawyers and said, "Counsel, approach the bench."

He placed his hand over the microphone in front of him as the two lawyers made their way in his direction. When they were assembled in front of him, he spoke in a soft but firm voice.

"Gentlemen," he said, "I don't know why the two of you are in this courtroom for this two-bit trial, but since you are here, let me make one thing clear. This will not be the trial of the century, and we need to move this case along. Peabody, get to the point, and make sure the witnesses you call do the same. Raker, we are all proud of how well you know the rules of criminal procedure, but if you make a hearsay objection every time one comes up, this trial will last a week. You need to swallow those objections and trust the fact that this Court will consider only competent evidence in rendering its verdict. If you don't like the result, you can ask for a jury trial. It won't hurt my feelings one bit, because if this trial ever ends, I will be retired. Are we clear?"

They both said "yes, your honor," and then turned and went back to their respective tables to continue the battle.

Peabody buttoned his coat, pressed it down in front of him and resumed his questioning.

"Ms. Barker, the Court would like to hear in your own words, exactly what you saw happen that night at the Tipsy Tavern."

Ms. Barker thought she had won the lottery. She looked over at Judge Stark approvingly. She had heard his little lecture to the lawyers and thought he was on her side now.

"So, here's the deal," she said. "The defendant and the woman got into an argument. It was pretty obvious she wanted something from him because—"

"Ms. Barker," Peabody said, interrupting her as politely as he could. "We need to be careful not to speculate about the state of mind of the victim," with the emphasis on the word victim.

"I am not specu—, that is, I am not making this up," she said. "She wanted something from him, and at first, she tried reasoning with him, but when that didn't work, she started complimenting him, saying how nice he looked in that red shirt. I mean, really? The shirt was as silly looking then as it is today."

There was muffled laughter in the courtroom, but no outburst and no admonishment from Judge Stark, just a muted smile on his face. Peabody was getting what he deserved with this witness. She had been on the stand for fewer than fifteen minutes, had said nothing specific about what had happened and had raised huge doubt about whether Peabody even had a victim. By saying nothing at all, Judge Stark was saying, let the chips fall where they may.

But Peabody was good. He didn't let this slow start get to him and he didn't break stride. If anything, it ramped up his game.

"Ms. Barker, it may help the Court if I orient you."

"You're going to do what to me?"

"Never mind," he said. "Did you see the victim, the woman behind me, fall down that night?"

"Yes, she fell down. In fact, she hit the floor hard on her back, and her knees rolled up like the drumsticks on a Thanksgiving turkey."

There were smiles in the courtroom but Peabody seemed unfazed. "What was she doing immediately before she fell?"

"She was standing face to face with the defendant. Both of them had gotten off their bar stools and they were having words."

"So he was close to her?"

"Yep," she said with a bit of frustration, as if Peabody hadn't heard her. For good measure, she added, "It looked to me like they was bosom buddies."

Peabody shifted gears. "What did you see as she was falling? Was the defendant near her then, too?"

"It looked that way to me. He was kind of leaning toward and over her."

"Kind of like he had just pushed her?" Peabody asked.

"Objection, your honor." Raker seemed to have gone missing in action since the attorney conference at the bench.

"Sustained," Judge Stark said.

"I will withdraw the question." Peabody turned back to the witness.

"Ms. Barker," Peabody asked, "can you tell the Court what happened next?"

"Sure. It was like the Friday Night SmackDown. After the victim, as you call her, fell down, she starting making noise like her ..."

Barker caught herself, remembering the last time she was rebuked for her "pants on fire" analogy. "Well, anyway," she went on, "given the noise she was making, you would have thought she had fallen out of a two-story window. Two good Samaritans at the bar came to her rescue. One of them went to comfort her. The other one grabbed the defendant and wouldn't let him leave. The bartender called 911, and in about five minutes, the cops showed up. That was pretty much it, except for the constant screaming and shouting of your victim, as you call her. She kept shouting 'I need it back.' "

"Did she appear to have any injuries?" Peabody asked, trying to get his witness back on track.

Ms. Barker thought about this for a moment, and then said, "I do remember that she was holding the back of her head after it was all over, and it looked like she had scraped the side of her face. Of course, it was hard to tell, because her face was bright red and her hair looked like she had stuck her finger in a socket."

"What did you do next?" Peabody asked.

"I made the mistake of telling a police officer what I saw."

"No further questions, your honor," Peabody said to Judge Stark.

"Cross-examination, Mr. Raker?" Judge Stark asked.

"Thank you, your honor. I have just a few questions. Ms. Barker, I want to thank you for coming down here today. I know it must have been inconvenient of the State to make you do so. I will not keep you here very long. Did you see my client, Henry Edmonds, who is seated next to me, actually hit the woman who is seated behind Mr. Peabody?"

"Nope," Barker said, "I did not."

"Did you see him raise his hand or fist toward her in any way?"

"Nope." Barker was warming up to Raker's style of questioning, short and to the point.

"I have just one last question, Ms. Barker. Is it true that you did not see my client push her?"

"True. I didn't see that either," Barker said.

"Thank you, Ms. Baker. You have been a wonderful witness. Those are all the questions I have."

"Ms. Barker," Judge Stark said, "you may step down." Turning back to Peabody, he said, "How many more witnesses do you have in this precedent-setting case of yours, Mr. Peabody?"

"Just two more witnesses, your honor. We plan to call the police officer and then finish our case with the victim, Ms. Judy Robertson." Looking around the courtroom and then back at Judge Stark, he added, "The officer should have been here by now."

Judge Stark did not look happy with Peabody. He glanced at the clock on the wall and said, "We are going to take our lunch break early to give Mr. Peabody the opportunity to search for the State's next witness. Bailiff ..."

The bailiff, who was hard at work on a crossword puzzle, was startled by the judge's directive. Standing, he said, "All rise," and once again, everyone did just that. In the most official voice he could command, the bailiff said: "This Court will be in recess until 2:00 p.m."

Lunch break

Once the recess was announced, Peabody texted the police officer to make sure he knew when and where to show up after lunch. He wasted no time waiting on a reply, picking up his file and escorting Judy Robertson to an adjacent room to discuss her upcoming testimony.

Raker checked his smartphone for messages, spoke briefly with Edmonds and left by a side door. Edmonds grabbed his coat, but as he turned to leave, he accidentally made eye contact with the little man in the black suit. What Edmonds felt when he looked into those coal-black eyes made him stop walking, because the anger those eyes projected operated like a force field holding Edmonds in place. Seconds passed, and the little man dismissively broke eye contact, finished typing something on his computer, closed it, grabbed his briefcase and walked down the aisle and out the courtroom door. Edmonds waited briefly, and followed in his path.

Other than the little man in the black suit, there were only a few spectators in the courtroom when the bailiff announced the lunch break. At the start of the trial, a number of attorneys with cases on the docket had been present but when it appeared that the trial might last until Christmas, they had drifted out. Those attorneys still in the courtroom either had business with the clerk or orders to be signed. There was just one other spectator, a person named Austin Land.

For many years, Austin Land had been a practicing attorney, but after thirty years in battle as a civil trial lawyer, he decided to try something different. Because he liked writing, he took a job with the local newspaper, investigating and writing about legal disputes. As he explained it to himself, rather than continuing to swim around in a legal fishbowl, he would dry off and write about the fish.

With a seasoned judge and two overqualified lawyers on hand, Courtroom 3150 looked like the appropriate fishbowl to peer into for the day.

When Judge Stark left the courtroom, Land grabbed his laptop and headed to the corridor to do quick Internet research. He didn't understand why the State was wasting taxpayer money and the Court's time on this case. He wanted to know more.

Peabody had said there were only going to be two other witnesses for the State, the police officer and the victim, but the police weren't present when the crime went down. Given the dubious testimony of the lead-off witness, this left the State's victim as the only possible eyewitness to the alleged assault. Land knew from experience that when the only witness who can place blame on the defendant is the victim, the State has an uphill battle. It becomes the old "he said, she said" quagmire.

If this was Peabody's decision to prosecute, he was slipping, Land thought. Mr. Edmonds must have done something to cause the victim to press charges, but it didn't look like assault. And the alleged victim, Ms. Robertson, must have had some real pull to get the D.A. to prosecute a guy in what was shaping up to be a losing effort.

Land found a place down the hall to plug in his laptop. The bench seat attached to the wall was too far away from the plug, so turning his back to the wall, he simply slid down to the marble floor and flipped open the computer lid. He quickly powered up, and in a few minutes, he was searching away.

It didn't take him long to find information about Judy Robertson. She worked for the county tax department as director of revaluation, a title she received only a year earlier. Just before she got the position, the tax office had been in the news. The previous director had botched the county's effort to revalue all the real estate in the county. As a result, heads rolled, and Robertson's predecessor was out of a job. For the last year, she had been supervising a large staff of employees and an even larger group of contracted appraisers. But none of this answered the question on Land's mind, which was: Why had she gone to the Tipsy Tavern on 9th Street on November 20th?

Land dug around some more and found that she had an undergraduate degree in computer programming, finishing top in her class, and a graduate degree in business, with an emphasis in municipal government. Besides her successful career,

Robertson served on several non-profit boards. She seemed like an up-and-coming star in both local government and the non-profit world, which didn't match the personality of someone who frequents the Tipsy Tavern.

A few minutes later, Land found her name in an online newspaper article, trumpeting her volunteer work with the local Salvation Army's kettle campaign. That campaign requires a slew of people to stand by red kettles and ring bells for Christmas charity, but in recent years, kettle helpers were getting harder and harder to recruit. Robertson came up with an idea as to how to put more kettles on the street while at the same time helping people who had lost their jobs. She persuaded the business community to hire and pay unemployed adults to staff the kettles for the Salvation Army.

So, Land thought, during the day, Judy Robertson was out arranging work for the unemployed and raising money for a good cause, and at night, she was going to a bar on the seedy side of town, only to get knocked around by an old man in a red flannel shirt. Something didn't add up.

Just then, Land noticed, or rather felt, a shadow over him. Looking up from his seat on the floor, he saw a little girl sitting on the marble bench next to him, swinging her legs forward and back and smiling at him.

"You are looking in the wrong place," she said.

"Who are you, young lady, and why are you looking over my shoulder?" Land asked.

"It is not who I am that matters, now is it? Rather," she said, "I believe the better questions are, who is Mr. Edmonds and why he is being prosecuted. Don't you agree?"

Land eyed the young girl warily and then noticed, upon further reflection, that while she did have the qualities of youth and was small in stature, she had a maturity about her. He also noticed something else, something strange. Her ears had an odd, pointed shape to them, or so he thought. She had long blond hair that flowed wispily over her ears, so maybe he was imagining things. And yet, if he didn't know better, particularly given her green tights, curved-toe shoes, lacy top and felt hat, she could have been an elf who had just come from helping Santa Claus at the local mall.

Just then, the well-dressed little man walked by and looked in Land's direction. His expression was unfriendly, which didn't bother Land. He was used to that "mind your own business" look often given to reporters, but he did wonder why the man was there.

Land turned back to speak with the girl, but just like that, she was gone. He got up and looked around. Where did she go? And what did she mean by him looking in the wrong direction? Scratching his head, he asked himself another question: Why were a young girl who looked like an elf, a little man with a killer stare, the county's director of revaluation and the best assistant district attorney in the D.A.'s office, all interested in an old man in a worn red flannel shirt?

Land was perplexed. But he was also very interested. When a reporter who also happens to be a former lawyer gets interested in a case, chances are the riddle will be solved. Land felt he was the guy to do it.

Meanwhile, Assistant District Attorney Jason Peabody and Judy Robertson were talking strategy while eating sandwiches ordered from the courthouse deli. The room they were in was decorated in old courthouse fashion, meaning it was pretty nondescript, with a table, four chairs and no windows, but it served its purpose.

"Judy," Peabody said, "you still haven't told me why this case is so important to you, and I am beginning to have my doubts that Judge Stark will think much of our evidence. You have to give me more to go on. What else can you tell me?"

Robertson sighed. "Jason, I really appreciate you taking on this case for me, but there are certain things that are too hard to explain. I can tell you this: The information on that flash drive belongs to the county and we must get it back. You are a good lawyer and I know you will figure out a way to do just that."

"But why go to all this trouble, with a criminal case, and why make this so public? Why not just offer the guy some beer money for the thing? From the looks of him, I doubt he will turn you down."

Robertson paused, dabbed at the corner of her mouth with her napkin and put her sandwich down. "Jason, you don't know him like I do. He may look like a homeless man in search of his next drink, but he is something entirely different."

"OK," Peabody responded, "whatever you say, but can you at least tell me enough so I can cross-examine the guy? Otherwise, Judge Stark is going to find him not guilty and let him keep the flash drive."

Robertson answered Peabody's question with a question. "Where is the flash drive now?"

Peabody was a bit frustrated by her change of course. "It's evidence. The officer took the device off

Edmonds at the scene and will bring it with him when he testifies. It will be our job to prove it belongs to the county."

She was silent for a moment, and Peabody broke in on her train of thought. "So what will it be, Judy?" Peabody asked. "Do I have to make this case up as I go along, or are you going to give me at least a hint about the facts?"

She thought to herself, made a decision and then told Peabody what she hoped would be enough to appease him.

When she was finished, he said, "You have got to be kidding."

Meanwhile, a few blocks down the street, Thad Raker was in his law office looking at an envelope that had been hand-delivered to his office. It was thin and had no return address. He slipped a letter opener along the top of the envelope and found a short letter addressed to Thad Raker, Esquire, with a reference caption that read: "The Edmonds trial." The letter read:

> Dear Mr. Raker:
> By now, additional funds have been deposited in your firm's trust account sufficient to cover your fee in the case. Because we doubt that Mr. Edmonds will be much help to you in his

> defense, enclosed is a list of questions that you may find useful in examining Ms. Robertson and Mr. Edmonds. We want the flash drive more than we want the truth, primarily because few people will believe the truth. We thank you for your continued discretion in the handling of this matter.

This was the second letter that had been hand-delivered to Raker in the last three days, and, like the first letter, it was unsigned.

He sat back in his desk chair, looked out the window and thought to himself. It had only been seven days since he received the call about representing Mr. Edmonds and when he got the call, he was a little uncertain about taking the case, because the caller was not the defendant, and because the caller refused to identify himself. Thus, Raker had asked for a high fee, along with the requirement of a significant deposit, thinking that the caller would go elsewhere. But he didn't. Instead, Raker received the deposit with the first letter, and now, looking at the latest letter in his hand, he had more than enough money to cover the time he would spend on the case.

Nonetheless, Raker felt uncomfortable. Mr. Edmonds was tight-lipped about the facts and Mr.

Edmonds' anonymous benefactor appeared to have a goal that might not be the same as his client's. It was a highly unorthodox way to litigate a case, and Raker would not have taken it but for his pressing financial situation.

Raker took a look at the two-page list of questions that came with the letter and after doing so, he thought to himself that this was a strange case indeed.

Henry Edmonds, meanwhile, was sitting in his Ford pickup truck in a parking lot near the courthouse, looking out the driver's side window and thinking about the mess he had gotten himself into, when he suddenly felt the presence of someone else. Turning his head to the right, he saw the same little girl who had engaged Austin Land in conversation.

"Hello, Henry," she said, smiling.

"You shouldn't be here," he said. "This is my problem, not yours, and if they think you are mixed up in this, it could affect your career."

"Oh, Henry, you know that I can't turn my back on a friend, and a true friend you are indeed. You have been so good to me over the years and I would like to help you," she said.

"I am beyond help, and you know it," Edmonds said. "What I did is contrary to the rules of the

Collection Code and unless I can fix this problem, the county jail will be the least of my problems."

"You let your heart get the better of you and things simply got out of control. Some of those rules, especially the new ones, are just silly."

"That is not how the task force will see it," Edmonds replied. "I took an oath to do this job according to its requirements, including any amendments to the rules, and all they care about is the flash drive. They plan to cut me loose."

"I will not leave you alone and all is not lost. We will figure a way to solve this problem, help you keep your job and maybe even convince the boss that the recent changes were ill-conceived." She put her hand on his arm. "You do want to keep your job, don't you?"

Henry Edmonds looked down and was quiet for a moment. He then turned and looked at his companion. "I wouldn't know what to do if I couldn't continue this work," he said.

"Then it's settled. You will not pout any longer, you will allow me to help you and you will begin helping yourself. You can start by getting back to the courtroom on time so they don't send the sheriff's deputy out to arrest you."

With that, Edmonds looked at his watch, and saw that he needed to get moving. When he turned to say goodbye to the little girl, he saw nothing but an empty seat.

Edmonds smiled. And then he gathered himself, and headed back to court.

Along the way, Henry Edmonds was met in the hallway by a stranger. "My name is Austin Land," the man said. "May I have a moment of your time?"

"I'm sorry, sir, but I can't be late to court."

"Look," Land said, not to be avoided, "I am an investigative reporter. Maybe I can help you with your case, if you just tell me why you and Ms. Robertson were meeting in a bar on 9th Street."

Edmonds laughed. "The location of our meeting is not what this case is about, and there is nothing a newspaper reporter can do that will help me in this case."

Not to be outflanked, Land said, "Come now, Mr. Edmonds, you know what they say about the power of the pen!"

"Yep, I do, but this is not a fight that can be won with a pen." Edmonds started to walk away.

"Wait," Land pressed, "at least tell me why I can't find anything out about you. You don't have a permanent job, you don't have a criminal record, you don't have a family, you don't have a home; in fact," Land remarked, rather incredulously, "it's as if you don't even exist, and that can't be, because I am looking right at you. Who are you, really?"

"That's easy, sir," Edmonds said, "I am the defendant and I have to get back to court."

Land followed him close behind.

Farther down the hallway, the little man was watching Land and Edmonds. When they separated, he too headed back to the courtroom.

2:00 p.m.

The bailiff stood by the clerk's desk as the courtroom began to come back to life.

Edmonds took his seat by Raker and listened distractedly to what his lawyer whispered in his ear. Across the aisle, Peabody sorted through the papers in front of him and Robertson settled in her seat, readying herself for what was to come. And then the door opened and Judge Stark entered.

"Stay seated, and come to order," the bailiff said, "this Court is back in session."

"Call your next witness." Judge Stark flopped into the big chair behind his bench.

"The State calls Officer Robert Charger," Peabody said.

"Fine, fine," Judge Stark said. "Officer Charger, you've been here before and you know the drill, so step on up here, take your seat and let's get on with it."

"Yes, sir," Officer Charger said.

Peabody started off with questions designed to build up the witness, asking him about his years on the police force, his upcoming promotion from patrolman to sergeant, some honors he recently received and other questions doing nothing but giving Judge Stark a headache.

Finally, Judge Stark was flummoxed enough. "Mr. Peabody," he said, "if you don't get to the point here, I will start to wonder whether Officer Charger is running for police chief rather than being the officer on call in this particular case."

"Yes, your honor, I just thought—"

"Well, you thought wrong. I know Officer Charger is an upstanding representative of the police shield in this fine community. Would it be too much to ask of you to simply have him ... Never mind." Judge Stark swung his chair toward Officer Charger. "Officer, we are going to cut right to the chase here. Tell us everything you know."

Officer Charger, who didn't particularly like lawyers to begin with, smirked a bit at Peabody's misfortune and got right to it.

"I was patrolling the West End when I got a call about a disturbance at the Tipsy Tavern. I called for backup and drove straight to the scene. It only took me a few minutes to get there and when I arrived, the defendant, the man in the red shirt," pointing at Edmonds, "was being cornered by two men, who were helping the woman over there." This time Officer Charger pointed to Robertson.

"When my backup arrived, I conducted interviews." Looking at his incident report, he continued. "I first spoke with the witness you heard from earlier, and then I spoke with the two men, but after learning that they didn't witness the altercation, I let them leave. I then spoke with the victim, Ms. Robertson, who had a lot of information to share."

"Well, go on," Judge Stark said, "let's hear what she told you," daring Raker to object on grounds of hearsay.

"She told me that the defendant had stolen property in his possession, a flash drive that belonged to the county, and that when she confronted him about it, he became physical."

"If I may, your honor?" Peabody asked.

"Oh, go ahead," Judge Stark responded.

"Officer Charger," Peabody asked, "could you describe Ms. Robertson's physical appearance and condition at the time?"

"She looked a little banged up. Her blouse was torn. She had a bruise on the side of her face and the back of her head had a bump on it, probably from when she hit the floor when defendant pushed her," Charger said.

"Objection," Raker said, "and move to strike. Officer Charger has no way of knowing whether Ms. Robertson was pushed, or whether she tripped or fell on her own."

"Ah, welcome back, Mr. Raker," Judge Stark said, "and thank you for that evidentiary lesson. Unfortunately, I have to agree with you." Turning toward Peabody, he said, "Sustained."

Peabody continued. "Officer Charger, tell us what you did when you learned that there may have been a theft."

"I searched the defendant for the flash drive."

"Did you find it, and, if so, what did you do with it?" Peabody asked.

"Yes, I found it. He had it in the front breast pocket of his red flannel shirt. So I bagged it, tagged it and logged it in as evidence when I booked the defendant."

"And did you bring it with you today?" Peabody asked.

Officer Charger said that he did, which resulted in Peabody marking and offering the flash drive as Exhibit 1 in the case of the State v. Henry Edmonds. Judge Stark accepted it into evidence, without objection by Raker, and then asked to see it.

When the flash drive was in his hand, Judge Stark pushed the knob that opened the male end and asked what was on it. Officer Charger explained that forensics had not been able to open the device because it was password-protected.

"In fact," the officer said, "every time forensics tried a password that failed, a video of a small Santa Claus showed up on the screen, holding his belly and laughing, until a few seconds later, when the Santa Claus leaned forward, and shook his white gloved index finger on his right hand from side to side, with a little crooked smile on his face, as if to say, 'you best behave.' "

Judge Stark looked at Officer Charger, not knowing exactly how to interpret this last piece of information. He returned the device to the evidence baggie and motioned for Peabody to continue.

"Did the defendant admit to assaulting Ms. Robertson and stealing the flash drive?" Peabody asked.

"He said he meant no harm," Officer Charger said, "which I took to mean he was sorry for his actions."

"Objection," Raker said, "that is pure speculation."

"Raker," Judge Stark said, "don't you think I know he is speculating? Give me some credit." Then, Judge Stark turned his attention to Officer Charger and told him to keep his opinions to himself.

"Just tell us what you learned," Peabody prompted.

"Well," Officer Charger said, "the defendant was silent about the flash drive and the victim insisted it belonged to the county, so that part of the case seemed pretty cut and dried. As for the pushing and shoving, the defendant admitted he grabbed her, but he denied pushing her, but with her statement, I felt that an arrest was warranted."

Peabody asked about the arrest and Officer Charger explained the details, including the precinct, time of day, amount of bail set, and the fact that bail was posted shortly after the arrest.

"That part was real interesting to me," Officer Charger said.

"What part?" Peabody asked.

"The part about how he got out so quick," Officer Charger responded. "I mean, he hadn't even been in long enough to make his first phone call, and the young girl out there," pointing to a girl sitting on one of the pews in the courtroom, "showed up and bailed him out. There is no way she could have known we had him that soon."

Hearing that, Austin Land, who had been busy typing on his laptop, perked up and looked around the room. In doing so, he found his target seated in the pew across the aisle from him. She was the same little girl who had spoken to him in riddles in the hallway. He wondered when she had slipped in and how she could have known so quickly that Edmonds had been arrested.

"Thank you," Peabody nodded to the defense attorney. "Your witness, Mr. Raker."

Raker stood up, asked permission to approach the witness and strode toward Officer Charger, scooping up Exhibit 1 on the way.

"Officer Charger," Raker began, holding the baggie by one end. "What is on this thing?"

"I told you, I don't know," he said.

"You don't know. Interesting." Raker looked at the device as he held it up, turning his gaze back to the officer. "But isn't this the 'cut and dried' part of the case?"

"That's right," Officer Charger said, a little uncertain.

"And yet, wouldn't you agree," Raker pressed the point, "that knowing what is on this thing, is exactly the kind of information that would be of great benefit to the Court in determining ownership? And if the information that is on this thing belongs to the defendant, or to an organization he works for, rather than to the county for whom Ms. Robertson works, don't you think that will change the 'cut and dried' nature of this case?"

"Objection," Peabody said, "There is no evidence in the record that the information belongs to the defendant or to an organization he works for, making this question purely hypothetical."

Before Judge Stark could rule, Raker withdrew the question, adding: "Your honor, my question may have been a hypothetical to this witness, but I respectfully submit that there are two key questions in this case: One, whether my client has a better claim to the flash drive than the county, and two, whether the so-called assault of Ms. Robertson is just a sideshow to conceal something far more sinister."

"Thank you for that jury speech, Mr. Raker," Judge Stark said. "Only there is no jury here today, as you well know. Anything else?"

Raker placed the Exhibit 1 baggie on the ledge in front of the witness box, turned around and walked back to his table.

"One more question," Raker said to the witness, as he turned back around. "Did it occur to you to ask Ms. Robertson, a high-ranking official in the county tax office, why she was meeting an older man she hardly knew in a bar on 9th Street?"

Officer Charger sat silent, thinking, but he came up with nothing in response.

"I thought so," Raker said. "Those are all the questions I have for this witness, your honor."

Judge Stark excused Officer Charger and told the lawyers to approach the bench. He gave them another lecture about moving the case along and reminded Peabody that he needed to provide some real evidence, saying that he assumed that whatever evidence Peabody had next would do the trick. And with that, he dismissed them back to their tables, with the advice that they remember where they were, in a court of law, a place that acts on evidence, not charade.

Peabody called Robertson to the stand and got right to work.

"State your name for the record, ma'am."

"Judy Robertson," she said. Her voice was clear and confident, although there weren't many people left in the courtroom to hear it. The bailiff and the clerk were there, because they had to be, but they were at best disinterested. To them, this was just another case in the People's Court. And then there were the three people left in the audience, Austin Land, the little girl and the little man. It was not much of a crowd.

Peabody asked Robertson where she had grown up and where she went to school. Then he asked her how she came to hold her current position with the county.

She explained the problems and bad press suffered by the county tax department due to the recent property tax revaluation. None of the values had been right, as they should have been, leading to late-night county commission meetings, scathing editorials in the newspapers, visits from politicians in the capital city and appeals from taxpayers that were going to create hearings long into the next revaluation cycle. It had been a real mess.

At Peabody's urging, she explained how she had gotten the department back on track, by creating a much deeper bench of independent contractor appraisers and developing a computer program to analyze the valuation problems neighborhood by neighborhood. As she was starting to explain the situation in more detail, Judge Stark broke in.

"Mr. Peabody, I am sure the few people in this courtroom appreciate, as much as I do, this stirring history lesson regarding this county's inability to enforce the *ad valorem* tax laws in an evenhanded manner, but Mr. Edmonds is not on trial for failing to pay his property taxes."

"Understood, your honor," Peabody said. "I just thought this foundation would be helpful to the Court to—

"Well, it's not helpful to the Court," Judge Stark said. "Move on!"

Peabody got to the point. "Ms. Robertson, why did you go to the Tipsy Tavern on November 20th of this year?"

"I went to the bar to find and speak with the defendant."

"And why did you seek him out?" Peabody asked.

"He had property that belonged to the county," she said.

"And what property was that?"

"The flash drive in that baggie right there," Robertson said, pointing to Exhibit 1 on the ledge in front of her.

"What happened when you approached the defendant that night?" Peabody asked.

"I asked him to give me the flash drive and he refused. I tried to reason with him, but he was not cooperating."

"What happened next?"

"Well, I noticed he had the flash drive in his front pocket, so I reached to get it back, and he became physical." Robertson paused. The memories came flooding back.

"Take your time. I know this must be difficult for you,"

After a few moments, she continued. "He grabbed me and threw me backward with such force that I fell hard on the floor and banged the back of my head on the leg of the pool table. It was very painful, causing me to come to tears, I am ashamed to say."

"No shame in that," Peabody said. "Were you scared?"

"I was," she said. "He was much bigger and stronger. I was in a strange place and he was mentally unstable."

This prompted Raker into action. "Objection," he said, adding that the witness "is not an expert on the mental stability of my client."

Peabody jumped in. "Your honor, I agree she is not a doctor, but she can testify to facts that will allow the Court to make its own judgment about the mental capacity of Mr. Edmonds. We will tie this all together in just a moment."

Judge Stark looked at the clock on the wall, and said, "Fine, Mr. Peabody, but you better get on with it, because we will not be holding court on Christmas Day."

The testimony that followed made the case more interesting, even to the bailiff and the clerk. Peabody asked Robertson to go back in time to when she first met Edmonds and tell the tale forward and what a tale it was.

"I met Mr. Edmonds in November at a kettle worker orientation session when I was helping the Salvation Army," Robertson said. She explained that he was hired to work a kettle job on 9th Street, just a block east of the Tipsy Tavern, and near the uptown bus station. "He came up to me and introduced himself, and I found him to be a nice old man, who looked rather down on his luck," she said. "I had no idea what was coming."

Peabody asked, "What do you mean?"

Robertson paused, looked down at her hands, and then up at Judge Stark. He looked back, waiting.

"He told me the most interesting, unbelievable story I have ever heard," she said.

Even Judge Stark looked mildly interested.

Robertson began and didn't stop until she told it all.

"Mr. Edmonds told me he wanted to work for the Salvation Army, because he liked playing Santa Claus and he liked helping people. He said he had a regular job working as a collector. I think he said he was a Collector, First Class. I asked him if he was a tax collector, and he just laughed. He said what he collected had nothing to do with taxes.

"He told me he had something that would help me in my revaluation work for the county. He didn't say how he knew what I did for a living, but I continued to listen."

Robertson described the conversation as cordial. Edmonds complimented her on the work she was doing to help the underprivileged and said he appreciated how she was trying to make things right for the county's taxpayers. He said he knew how hard it was to get reliable information on the size, layout and dimensions of properties and he wanted to help her, because she was helping others. He told her he had detailed information on every house in the county.

"How he had such information was a mystery to me," Robertson said. "I saw the old truck he drove and the clothes he was wearing. He looked then about the way he looks today, with the same red flannel shirt and worn appearance. Gathering the type of information he described would be a tremendous undertaking. I began to wonder if he might have obtained the information improperly.

"He then showed me a flash drive and said that a database with the information I needed was on it. He said he would share it with me if I would help him with another database on the flash drive, and this is when things got a little odd," Robertson said.

"He told me there were three databases on the flash drive. One database contained all current information on the physical features of every home in the county. He called it the property database and said it would give me everything I needed to bring closure to the county's tax revaluation process in record time. He did not need my help with that database, he said. Nor did he need my help on what he called The Archives.

"It was the second database, the one he called the evaluation database, that was his concern, but before he told me what was in the database, he asked me whether he could trust me to be discreet.

I asked him if the database was used to evaluate real estate, but he shook his head no, saying the database was used for evaluations of an entirely different kind."

"Did he say anything else about the evaluation database before disclosing its contents?" Peabody asked.

"He said the child in me would understand why the computer program used to run that database needed to be fixed, but he didn't explain what he meant."

"And so you told him you would cooperate with him?" Peabody asked.

Rather apologetically, Robertson turned and said specifically to Judge Stark, "I didn't mean to mislead him, but I was curious, so I told him he could trust me. And when I did, he told me the story that led us here today."

"Well don't keep us in suspense, Ms. Robertson," Judge Stark said. "What was the story he told you that brought us here today?"

Stopping to gather herself, and then looking directly at the defendant, Robertson said: "Mr. Edmonds thinks he works for Santa Claus."

"You mean, of course, as an employee of the Salvation Army?" Judge Stark asked.

"No, sir," Robertson responded. "I mean, he thinks he works for the one and only Santa Claus, the one who lives at the North Pole."

Everyone in the courtroom but Raker looked toward Henry Edmonds, who was just sitting there, looking straight at Robertson. Raker was making notes, as if nothing unusual had happened.

Peabody had been letting this evidence soak in, when Judge Stark broke the silence: "Do you have any more questions for this witness, Mr. Peabody?"

"Yes, your honor," and after once again straightening and pressing his coat in front of him, he looked to Robertson.

"Ms. Robertson, did you receive and examine the flash drive?" Peabody asked.

"I did," she said. "Mr. Edmonds gave me the flash drive, along with the passwords to access the property and evaluation databases. He did not give me the password to access The Archives."

"And what did you find?"

"The first thing I noticed, upon a closer inspection, was that this was no ordinary flash drive. It did more than just hold data. It was able to receive information wirelessly and it had a mini-processor built into it with sophisticated programming. This was the most powerful small computer I had ever seen and it looked like a simple flash drive.

"The property database was exactly as he described. It contained helpful details on every home in the county, and it was not just a few details. These were the kind of details one gets only with an up-close inspection of the property. It described the square footage of each room, and it had a precise floor plan of the entire living space, showing entrance and exit points and even describing the locations of the fireplaces."

"What about the evaluation database?" Peabody asked.

"It was very suspicious. Mr. Edmonds had explained it to me, but when I looked at it, I couldn't believe what I was seeing."

"And why is that?" Peabody asked.

"That database listed the names and ages of the children occupying each home," she said. "When I saw it, I became worried as to how a man, who looked like a drifter, had a list with such specific information about every child in the county. I was worried that he might be gathering the information for an improper purpose."

"Did he tell you the purpose?"

"He did," Robertson replied, "but I didn't believe him."

"So, Ms. Robertson, what was Mr. Edmonds' explanation for having in his possession a database with the names, ages and places of residence for every child in the county?"

"You won't believe me if I tell you."

Judge Stark jumped in. "Ms. Robertson, just tell us what he said."

"He said he was working for Santa Claus, collecting information needed for the Naughty and Nice lists."

"Did he appear to be serious?" Judge Stark asked.

"Very much so. He went into great detail as to how the collection efforts worked in the past and how they work today and he seemed to believe every word of what he said. Apparently, due to the continuing expansion of the world population, the North Pole made a decision to implement ..." She stopped for a moment, and then said, without looking in the direction of the defendant, "Look, I am just conveying what he told me. I don't for a minute believe a word he said, but I will tell you what I heard."

"Continue," Judge Stark said.

"According to Mr. Edmonds," she said, "the North Pole collects behavioral data on children around the world by breaking the Christmas Grid, as he called it, into Christmas zones. Each Christmas zone is divided into Christmas districts, which is where the collectors do their work. The data collected in the Christmas Grid became so extensive that the North Pole started using computer technology about three years after personal computers were introduced to the public. The North Pole has had the technology for hundreds of years, but Mr. Edmonds said that Santa Claus was reluctant to use it until absolutely necessary because elves are even slower to accept change than regular people."

The clerk and bailiff were listening to this testimony with amused expressions on their faces. Judge Stark was listening, but he was anything but amused.

Robertson sensed that her words were going nowhere fast. "The point is that the defendant thinks he works for a make-believe boss, collecting information for make-believe Naughty and Nice lists."

"And what help did he need from you with respect to the lists?" Peabody asked.

"He told me," Robertson said, "that certain people in management at the North Pole had made a gift-giving policy change that was rather harsh. They did it by modifying the computer program used to generate results for the Naughty and Nice lists. Mr. Edmonds was insistent that Santa Claus knew nothing about it and would not have supported the change. He wanted to speak up, he said, but he was threatened with termination if he complained." She paused for breath.

"He wanted me to come up with a way to override the new computer program imbedded in the evaluation database," she said.

"To what end?" Peabody asked.

"His words?" she asked back.

"Yes," Peabody said.

"To save Christmas!"

The courtroom was quiet, except for the sound of Judge Stark tapping his pen on the pad in front of him.

Sensing doubt in the courtroom, Robertson volunteered some information. "He was serious about it. He believed what he was saying and I believed that he believed what he was saying. But it was all too ... well ... just too insane. He told me that unless we fixed the problem with how the evaluation database recorded who was Naughty and who was Nice, more than 30,000 children in this county would be treated unfairly, labeled as Naughty, simply because the powers that be did not have the heart to behave in a more equitable way. He said he had no sway, no power and no standing to reach high enough in the organization to effect the change, so he wanted me to help him. Together, he said, he and I could save Christmas for the good children of this county."

"What happened next?" Peabody asked.

"He gave me custody of the flash drive for the next five days. He said I could copy the information on the property database to help the county with its tax revaluation process and in return, I said I would take a look at the computer program on the evaluation database."

"You've said you didn't believe what he told you," Peabody said. "Why did you imply that you would help him?"

"I wanted to find out more about the property database," she said. "At that point, I thought he might have stolen the information. And I was worried about what he might do with the list of children, especially since it showed where they lived."

"So, Ms. Robertson," Peabody asked, "would you explain to the Court how you ended up at the Tipsy Tavern in a confrontation with the defendant?"

"After Mr. Edmonds gave me the flash drive, things went well for the first few days. The information on the property database proved to be as helpful as he promised but it was going to take at least five days to copy and integrate the data into our system. But we also found that a lot of the information already was in our files, leading our technicians to believe that the matching information was stolen from the county. We supposed that other information was gathered surreptitiously from other sources. I was just about to turn the whole matter over to the police when the flash drive disappeared."

"What do you mean?" Peabody asked.

"On the third day of our investigation, I checked the safe where I kept the flash drive, and it was gone. In its place was a note from Mr. Edmonds, saying he had changed his mind about me. Our original plan had been to meet on the fifth night at the Tipsy Tavern close to where he did his Salvation Army work, so I went there the next two nights, hoping to see him. On the fourth night, I found him, and here we are."

"Tell the Court what happened that night, Ms. Robertson."

She took a breath, and remembering back to that night, said, "He wouldn't listen to reason. I told him that the information on the flash drive had to be county property, and he needed to turn it over to me, or I would go to the police. As for the information on the children, I questioned him directly as to why he would be carrying such information. It was shady, I told him, which made him extremely angry. When I saw the flash drive in his pocket, I took my chance to get it, which is when he grabbed me and threw me to the floor."

"Why have you come forward to prosecute the defendant?" Peabody asked.

Robertson hesitated. When she tried to speak again, her voice cracked.

With the Court's permission, Peabody approached Robertson with a glass of water. She took it, thanked him and lifted her head.

"I will never forget the last words he spoke to me when I was on the floor. He told me that when I was a little girl, I had a tender, caring heart, but it was no longer tender or caring, and he was saddened by the change and disappointed in the person I had become. I had no idea what he meant and was frightened by the statement. How could he have known me as a girl? I didn't know this man until I met him last month at the Salvation Army center. It made me think again about the list of children he had on the flash drive and then I was even more scared. I came to court to recover the flash drive for the county and because I was concerned that someone else would get hurt unless the Court puts Mr. Edmonds behind bars."

Peabody let the uncomfortable silence in the courtroom linger for a few moments, turned to Judge Stark and said: "I have no further questions, your honor."

"Cross-examination, Mr. Raker?" Judge Stark asked.

"Just a few questions, Judge."

Defendant Edmonds leaned over and whispered something in Raker's ear, and after Raker listened, he stood up and said, "Judge Stark, on second thought, I have no questions for this witness."

Judge Stark stared at him for what seemed like a full minute. The victim had just accused Raker's client of stealing county property, causing personal injury and holding himself out as one of Santa's real helpers, and even so, Raker was not going to ask the victim any questions. Raker could feel the judge's disapproval, and expected to be summoned to the bench for a scolding. Finally, Judge Stark turned to Peabody and asked if he had any more witnesses.

"Yes, sir," Peabody answered. "The State would like to call Henry Edmonds."

In a flash, Raker was on his feet, but before he could speak, the judge held up a hand to stop him.

"Mr. Peabody," Judge Stark said, "did you flunk your class in constitutional law? Surely you are aware of a little set of rules we go by around here called the Bill of Rights, and in particular, the Fifth Amendment to the United States Constitution, which, as I hope you know, prevents a criminal defendant from being a witness against himself."

"I am aware of that, your honor," Peabody said, "but I thought Mr. Edmonds may want to answer a few questions, so we can move this case along, as you suggested earlier."

Judge Stark was not amused. "Mr. Peabody," he said, "my desire to move this case along does not mean that we are going to start trampling on the constitutional rights of the accused."

While this exchange was going on, Land noticed that Edmonds was in conversation with Raker who was shaking his head vehemently in the negative. This went on until Judge Stark took notice.

"Mr. Raker," Judge Stark asked, "are we interrupting something?"

Raker stood up, looked at his client, and said, "Your honor, it appears that my client is unwilling to accept my advice. Accordingly, I must ask the Court for permission to withdraw as counsel."

"Denied," Judge Stark said, as quickly as he could get the word off his lips. "You will not get out of this case that easily." He fixed his gaze on the defendant. "Mr. Edmonds, you have a good attorney, and you need to listen to his advice."

"I am ready to testify, Judge," Edmonds said.

"You will get your chance, should you decide to put on a case in your defense," Judge Stark said, "but right now, we are finishing with the State's case."

"I am not afraid to answer Mr. Peabody's questions," Edmonds said. "The clock is ticking. It will be Christmas soon, and I would like to get this resolved in time."

Suddenly, from the back of the courtroom, a voice broke in: "May it please the Court." The little man was on his feet, walking down the aisle.

"Who are you," Judge Stark asked, "and why are you interrupting my trial?"

"I am Hank Snow, and I am a security officer working for the CSTF."

"What the heck is the CSTF?" Judge Stark asked.

"It is the Christmas Security Task Force." Snow said.

"Let me guess," Judge Stark said, "you also work for Santa Claus, and you and Frosty the Snowman are prepared to vouch for the defendant."

"Far from it, your honor," Snow said. "I am prepared to reveal the truth about Mr. Edmonds, and provide proof that he is not the owner of the flash drive."

At this point, Peabody sensed an opening. "Your honor," Peabody said, "I would like to withdraw my request to call Mr. Edmonds as a witness and call Mr. Snow as the State's next witness."

"Very well." Judge Stark sounded resigned to fate. "It is obvious we won't finish today, so we will be in recess until 9:30 in the morning." And with that, he banged his gavel on the bench, grabbed his notes and left the courtroom, leaving the bailiff without enough time to announce his departure. But he did his best: "This Court will be in recess until 9:30 tomorrow morning. God save this State and this honorable Court."

Peabody tried to approach Snow, but Snow put up his hand. "I will talk tomorrow, not today, but I can assure you that you will have the evidence you need to put Mr. Edmonds in jail and prevent him from keeping the flash drive." And with that, Snow strode toward the exit.

Austin Land ran after him and intercepted him at the door.

"Mr. Snow," Land said, "it appears you know how to make both an entrance and an exit."

Snow eyed him with a glare as unfriendly as the one he had given to Peabody. "You don't know what you are playing with here. If you want to destroy Christmas, then go ahead and write about this trial. But if you want to preserve Christmas, you will write nothing about what you see or hear in this trial."

And with that he was gone.

"He is not really a bad person," the little girl said. She startled Land once again.

"Where did you come from?" he asked.

"From over there," she responded, pointing.

"How do you know Mr. Snow?" he asked.

"I can't tell you that, at least not yet," she said. "What I can say is that you should write what you observe and what you feel, but most of all, you should write what you believe." And with that she was out the door.

Land stepped to the hallway, walked to and caught the elevator and traveled to the first floor, all the while deep in thought. Suddenly, he had an idea and smiled to himself. He took out his smartphone, accessed his Twitter account and sent this message:

Austin Land @ALandReporter Dec. 23
Trial of the Century in the People's Court. #courtroom3150

One minute later he sent another tweet, saying:

> **Austin Land** @ALandReporter Dec. 23
> Evidence suggests Naughty and Nice lists hacked. #courtroom3150

One minute later he sent another tweet, saying:

> **Austin Land** @ALandReporter Dec. 23
> Santa's helper on trial. #courtroom3150

And then, one minute later, he sent another tweet, saying:

> **Austin Land** @ALandReporter Dec. 23
> Court's ruling could halt Christmas for thousands. #courtroom3150

When Land got home, he did even more to stir the pot. He added an article to his online newspaper blog, with the headline: "Trial of the Century in Courtroom 3150: Christmas is on the Line." It read:

> Today was a unique day in the People's Court, but few people were present to witness the action.
>
> The defendant on trial is Henry Edmonds, a man accused of being crazy, because he purports to be a helper of Santa Claus, as if that is a crime. The prosecution certainly thinks so, because the State wants him in jail, with Christmas just a day away.

But that is not the worst of it. The State is seeking to have the Court take from Mr. Edmonds a flash drive containing the Naughty and Nice lists and give it to the county tax collector. Imagine that, the Naughty and Nice lists in the possession of the tax collector, rather than Santa Claus. Talk about a lump of coal in your stocking.

And yet, all is not lost, because the trial continues. The odds may be against Mr. Edmonds, but he will have his final day in court tomorrow, even if he has no supporters.

The case kicks off at 9:30 a.m. on Christmas Eve and Santa's helper needs your assistance. He may be going to jail and his lists may fall into the wrong hands. If that means nothing to you, then stay home. Otherwise, see you in court.

32°

Bringing You the Latest News

DAILY NEWS Blog Post

December 23

Legal Affairs Blog Post

Trial of the Century in Courtroom 3150 - Christmas is on the Line

Today was a unique day in the People's Court, but few people were present to witness the action.

The defendant on trial is Henry Edmonds, a man accused of being crazy, because he purports to be a helper of Santa Claus, as if that is a crime. The prosecution certainly

Last Day Sale 40% OFF ALL CHRISTMAS ITEMS

Last Day Sale 40% OFF ALL CHRISTMAS ITEMS

7:30 p.m.

Judge Stark was at home with his wife, Kay, when something disturbing came to his attention. They had just finished their dinner and were settling into their evening routine of reading the daily news. His practice was to read the morning paper, because this was the time of day when he could read it cover to cover. Her practice was to stay more current, by relying on her tablet and the Internet to feed her the news. He tolerated her preferences, just as she did his.

They were about twenty minutes into their respective attention to the news, when she asked him the question.

"Dear," she said, "have you heard about the trial in Courtroom 3150?"

He put the paper down and looked at her as if she had just grown a mustache. She handed him her tablet so that he could see for himself. A moment later he was reading Austin Land's blog post, looking none too happy about it.

"I know more than I want to know about this trial, but unfortunately, I will know even more tomorrow, because I am the judge assigned to this case."

"So what are you going to do?"

"You know I can't talk about my cases," he said, "but if you must know, the defendant thinks he works for Santa Claus and there is the problem of a stolen flash drive. It doesn't look good for the defendant."

"Let me get this straight," she said. "You are eight days away from retirement, and you are going to decide in one of your last cases as judge to put Santa's helper in jail and turn the Naughty and Nice lists over to the tax department? Is that what I am hearing?"

Judge Stark snapped back. "You and everyone else should forget about the Santa Claus intrigue in this case. This is nothing more than a case of assault and larceny, in which I am required to perform my duty."

"Well, that's all well and good, Augustus, but, if you decide to convict the defendant, I hope our friends and neighbors, and, more importantly, our grandchildren, don't learn of your involvement, because they will care very little about your duty."

Judge Stark stood up. "I am going to bed early. This topic is making my head hurt and tomorrow could be a long day."

Meanwhile, Thad Raker was at dinner with his girlfriend, a beautiful schoolteacher named Elizabeth Foley, who could not be matched in this world, at least in his opinion. For the last six months, he had been thinking about asking her to marry him, but the financial strain of his law practice had caused him to delay that decision. Recently, however, because of the large fee he had received in the Edmonds case, he was giving the idea of marriage more thought. He just wished the money came without the ethical concerns.

His Elizabeth was a good listener, and it was that quality that led Raker to open up to her after dinner.

Raker explained that he was defending a case in which he had received a huge fee from an anonymous source, but the more the case progressed, the more it seemed like the source wanted his client to lose. The client, Mr. Edmonds, was a nice old man who did not appear to be the kind of person who would assault a female, steal personal property or lie about it. Raker wanted to help him, but he wasn't sure that he could, because Mr. Edmonds believed himself to be working for Santa Claus.

"What do you think I should I do?" he asked her.

Elizabeth was not only supportive, she was wise. She did not try to tell Raker what to do. Instead, she asked him to think about the lawyer in the movie, "Miracle on 34th Street," which they had watched together last Christmas. The lawyer defended a department-store Santa Claus in an insanity commitment proceeding, a case in which the defendant believed himself to be the one and only Santa. At long odds, the lawyer wins the case, and everyone lives happily ever after. The lawyer's girlfriend tells the department-store Santa Claus, when all seemed lost in the case, that she believes in him. Elizabeth said, "I believe in you, too." That was enough for Raker.

A conversation of another sort was taking place across town. Peabody thought Robertson had been holding something back from him so he had taken her to dinner to talk it out. He picked a restaurant close to her home, one that was quiet, so they would not be disturbed.

This was the first time Peabody and Robertson had been to dinner together in years. As children, they had been fast friends. They attended the same grade school, middle school and high school, where they had even dated a few times. But they parted ways when they went off to college.

Now the State's criminal case against Henry Edmonds had brought them together again. Although they had yet to admit it, they were discovering they still had feelings for each other.

"So how do you feel about prosecuting a man who thinks he works for Santa Claus?" Robertson asked.

"In all honesty, with Christmas just one day away, I would prefer not to have the job," he replied. "I suspect the press will have a field day with this case no matter how it turns out."

"Yes, I can see the headline now," she said: "Prosecutor Jason Peabody puts Santa's helper in jail"

"Don't forget the related article," he said: "Tax Office Takes Custody of Naughty and Nice Lists; Christmas in Peril." They both laughed.

They were silent for a moment, until Peabody asked, "Why didn't you tell me sooner about the Santa Claus part of this case?"

"I don't know," she said, "maybe I thought you wouldn't take the case."

"You know me better than that," he said. She clasped his hands in hers and said: "But there is more, Jason, and I am sorry I didn't tell you sooner."

For the next five minutes, Jason Peabody listened to Judy Robertson confide in him. And as she did, she cried. As he listened, he tried to comfort her, telling her that everything would be all right, but in reality, he didn't know whether that was true or not.

9:00 a.m.

Judge Stark was in his courthouse office trying to get his thoughts in order when he heard a knock on his door. It was a fellow jurist, Judge Robert Owens.

"Hey, Gus," Owens said, "after you sentence this guy, maybe you should be sure his cell doesn't have a chimney so his boss doesn't use it to break him out!"

"Very funny." Judge Stark had little desire to join in the joke.

"Or," said Owens, "you could let him out on work-release and place him in the custody of his boss, because Santa is going to need a lot of help tonight."

"Why don't I just take a sick day and let you take over?"

"No, siree," Owens said, "I don't want anything to do with this case. In fact, if you put this guy in jail and give the Naughty and Nice lists to the wrong party, I don't even want anyone to know I am your friend." At that, Owens laughed at his own joke, turned for the door and said, "Good luck, old friend." Judge Stark grunted and waved him away.

A minute later, Judge Stark heard a commotion in the hallway outside his door. When he went to investigate, he found three sheriff's deputies arguing about something.

"What seems to be the problem?" Judge Stark asked, with little patience.

"We need more security in Courtroom 3150 today, your honor," said one of the deputies.

"We need at least four deputies," another said.

"But we don't have that many to spare," another said.

"What are you talking about?" Judge Stark asked. "We only had three spectators in the courtroom yesterday afternoon and only needed one deputy."

At that point, all three deputies, none of whom wanted to be the one to break the news to Judge Stark, looked at each other and said nothing, and then the voices coming from the courtroom said what they failed to reveal. Judge Stark opened the back door to the courtroom and what he saw left him speechless.

Row upon row of spectator pews in the People's Court already had reached their capacity and others were filling up fast. It appeared that all ages were represented in the amassing throng, from young children to aged adults.

Elizabeth Foley was there, supporting Raker. She had come up with the brilliant idea to call the parents of a few children in her class and alert them to the civics lesson in progress. The parental grapevine spread the news quickly, resulting in more than twenty second-graders and their parents showing up to pull for Santa's helper.

Austin Land brought a number of people with him, too, including friends, newspaper employees and former colleagues in the legal profession.

Even court personnel with no business in 3150 were taking time from their work to see what the fuss was about.

And then there were the people who were just following the people, just to see what was going on.

In the far back right-hand corner, unbeknownst to Judge Stark, was his wife Kay.

9:25 a.m.

The courtroom was full, with no open seats. The three deputies had stopped squabbling and stepped into their places as bailiffs, one on each side, and one in the back. As the clock on the wall ticked closer to 9:30, they stood at attention and the conversation in the room dropped to a low electric ebb.

The door to the back hallway was cracked so one bailiff could see when Judge Stark was ready to enter, and when his robed figure appeared in the crack, that bailiff took charge. In a commanding voice for all to hear, he told the populace to stand and take notice that Courtroom 3150 was in session, with the Honorable Augustus Langhorne Stark, judge, presiding. Everyone was told to be seated and come to order.

What a difference it was from the day before. Yesterday afternoon, Judge Stark had been presiding over a near-empty courtroom, and now, he was staring at a People's Court full of people. His first order of business was to take control, telling everyone in attendance that they had a right to be there but they must behave themselves. He made it clear that he would not tolerate any disruptions, because, as he said, "this is a court of law, not a variety show." Those who did not comply with this directive would be escorted from the room. Those who were particularly unruly would be held in contempt of court and put in jail, and, with that, he slammed his gavel down, and told Peabody to call his next witness.

"The State calls Hank Snow."

Peabody looked around the room for the little man, but did not see him. Then he heard the sounds of a row of people standing to let someone pass before them, and when he looked in that direction, he saw Mr. Snow making his way down the row to the aisle. At the aisle, Snow buttoned his coat and swept his left hand down the front of his immaculate black suit. The only thing that hinted of friendliness in the man was his customary red tie. In his right hand, he held a file folder. He strode forward, pushed through the wooden gate and headed for the witness stand. On his way, he grabbed two of the bailiff's crossword puzzle books. He dropped them in the witness chair and jumped up on them to see over the witness ledge, ready to state his case.

After Snow was sworn in, Peabody got right to it. "Mr. Snow, yesterday you said that you had some information that will prove the case for the State, but before we get to that, please tell us about yourself and your employer."

Snow had a deep voice for a small man. "I work for an organization called North Pole Enterprises, LLC, a company formed under the laws of the State of Delaware."

"What is your position with that organization?" Peabody asked.

"Security."

"Can you elaborate?" Peabody asked.

"As I mentioned yesterday, I work for the CSTF, otherwise known as the Christmas Security Task

Force," Snow said. "I am the senior officer on the task force."

"And what is the job of the CSTF?" Peabody asked.

"Our job is to catch people like Mr. Edmonds and retrieve property that belongs to the company."

"I am not sure I follow."

"We are a multibillion-dollar international organization." Snow looked frustrated at having to explain things to Peabody. "Security is important; no, it is critical, especially around Christmas, because that's when the public depends upon our ability to deliver. We spend the entire year developing confidential shipping and delivery information, which we can hardly allow to be compromised. If something is stolen at this time of year, it could affect the whole operation."

"So you do not work for Santa Claus?" Peabody asked.

"Counselor," Snow said, looking into the audience of children before him, "I assume this case is about two things, whether a woman was assaulted and whether a man took something he should not have taken. Whether I work for the Easter bunny, the tooth fairy or Santa Claus should not matter to this Court."

With that, Judge Stark, who normally would come down hard on a sarcastic non-responsive witness, decided to let the man be, with grudging respect. Perhaps, thought Judge Stark, Mr. Snow could keep Santa Claus out of this case.

Peabody decided to move on as well. "Fair enough, Mr. Snow," Peabody said, "would you please tell the Court what evidence you have that is relevant to this case."

At that, Snow took the folder he was holding and pulled out several pieces of paper. "I hold in my hand," he said, "the bill of sale for the flash drive. It bears the serial number on the device, the date of purchase and the owner, which is North Pole Enterprises, LLC."

Peabody asked to approach the witness, permission was granted and he found himself standing before Mr. Snow, who then handed him the document. Looking it over, Peabody could tell it was official. He had Snow authenticate his signature and then offered the document into evidence, as Exhibit 2. Judge Stark took the document, looked it over, and announced that Exhibit 2 was admitted into evidence.

Peabody then noticed that Snow held a second document and asked him about it.

"This," Snow said, "is a confidentiality agreement signed by the defendant. It shows that the flash drive was delivered to him on December 26th of last year and it shows that he was to return the flash drive to us once his work was completed, on December 1st of this year. We needed it by that date to complete our work on or before December 25th."

Peabody looked at the document. The signer had acknowledged that the flash drive belonged to North Pole Enterprises, LLC, and that the signer was bound to keep its contents confidential, not share it with any third party, and return it as promised on the appointed date. The signature of the obligor was a bit hard to read, so Peabody asked Snow for help.

"Yes," Snow said, "I recognize the signature, and not only that, I witnessed the man sign the document. It is the signature of Henry Edmonds, the defendant in this case."

"That document will be accepted as Exhibit 3," Judge Stark said.

Peabody realized that while exhibits 2 and 3 would make it difficult for Edmonds to prove ownership of the flash drive, they also would make it hard for Robertson to retrieve the flash drive for the county, so he shifted his line of questioning to the information contained on the flash drive.

"Mr. Snow, these two documents suggest that the flash drive is owned by your company, but they do not demonstrate that the information which is on the flash drive belongs to your company. Can you tell the Court what information was on the flash drive when it was delivered to Mr. Edmonds on December 26th of last year?"

For the first time, Snow's wall of confidence appeared shaken, but only slightly. "We load all our flash drives with copyrighted spreadsheets and—"

"Let's back up a moment, Mr. Snow," Peabody said. "How about explaining to the Court how many flash drives are issued to your employees and what they are used for, because there seems to be some confusion about the purpose of the lists of children on the flash drive."

At the mention of the lists, there was excited whispering in the audience.

"Order." Judge Stark banged his gavel on the bench. "Everyone must remain quiet, so I can hear the evidence."

"The information is proprietary," Snow replied, "and for that reason, I cannot share it with you but I can explain the process."

"Go on," Peabody said.

"Each December 26th, flash drives are delivered to 15,000 employees around the world. They are collectors of information for the company, that is to say, for North Pole Enterprises, LLC, not for Santa Claus. In many respects, we are like Santa's helpers, because we can deliver what children want and when they want it, by Christmas morning. The lists, as you refer to them, even mimic the work of Santa Claus. It is true, there are Naughty and Nice lists, but they do not belong to Santa Claus. They are simply records of whether parents are going to buy toys for their children. We adopt the philosophy that if parents are planning to place an order, the children have been good. If no order is placed, the children have been bad."

Austin Land was in the audience taking notes on his laptop, but when he heard this piece of evidence, he took out his smartphone and sent a tweet to his followers:

> **Austin Land** @ALandReporter Dec. 24
> Witness blames Naughty and Nice decisions on parents. #courtroom3150

"Wait a minute," Peabody said, "if this company is as large and prosperous as you say, why is it that no one has heard of it, and what makes you so sure that if parents don't order from your company, their children have been bad?" Peabody asked.

"The reason no one knows about the company is because until now, our employees have honored their promise of confidentiality." Snow directed an angry glare at Edmonds. "With regard to the lists, our company has been doing this work for years, we have some well-tested methods and have rarely been wrong."

"Fine," Peabody said, "you are employed by a large company that does work similar to the work of Santa Claus, and you do a fairly good job of keeping secrets, but that doesn't prove your company owns the information that was put on this flash drive, with emphasis on the word 'information.' Why, for example, does a toy company need such detailed information on the homes in this county?"

"Counselor, I cannot reveal the trade secrets of my company concerning the confidential information on the flash drive. All I can say is the information we obtain helps us meet the needs of our clients, from the time an order is placed right up until the time it is delivered. If you think the information belongs to the tax department, then prove it."

Suddenly Judge Stark took control. "Mr. Snow you will act with respect in this courtroom, or you will not act here at all. Do you understand?"

Snow nodded, a thin line of contempt showing on his pressed lips.

Peabody was now worried. It was going to be difficult to prove that the flash drive or any information on it belonged to the county, and he was second-guessing his decision to call Snow as a witness. Yesterday, it sounded like Snow held the keys to success for the prosecution, but today, the case to recover the flash drive was slipping away. Maybe, thought Peabody, Snow could help on the assault charge.

"Mr. Snow," Peabody asked, "do you have any personal knowledge of what happened in the Tipsy Tavern between Ms. Robertson and Mr. Edmonds?"

"I do," Snow said. "I saw what happened."

"Please tell the Court what you saw," Peabody directed, hoping this line of questioning would be more fruitful.

"I saw Mr. Edmonds push Ms. Robertson to the floor. There is no doubt in my mind," Snow said.

"And why were you in the Tipsy Tavern that night?"

"Mr. Edmonds did not report in on his last check-in date, which triggered an internal alert. I was in the area, so I decided to investigate. On the night in question, I followed Mr. Edmonds to the bar and watched from across the room as he and Ms. Robertson talked. Then, when she stood up, he grabbed her and threw her to the floor. It was assault, I am sure of it."

"Thank you, Mr. Snow," Peabody said. "No further questions, your honor."

"Mr. Raker," prompted Judge Stark, "do you have any questions of this witness?"

Raker was deep in thought. That morning, he had received a strange text message, saying: "A large deposit has been made in your firm's trust account. Do not cross-examine Mr. Snow!" He had checked his bank account on his smartphone, and it was true. A large deposit had been received, so large that for the first time in his legal career, he would have the financial freedom to do what he wanted, which was to marry Elizabeth. At the same time, he had never done anything unethical in his law practice, and her words were still present in his mind. She believed in him, and she was here, in the courtroom, supporting him.

Raker was awakened from ruminating on his troubling dilemma by Judge Stark, who asked again whether he had any questions for the witness. Looking at his client, who depended on him, and knowing that Elizabeth was behind him, Raker said, "Yes."

Mr. Snow was none too pleased.

Raker decided that if the prosecution was going to use his client's belief in Santa Claus against him, he would try to turn the tables.

"Mr. Snow," Raker said, with a little of his own sarcasm, "is it just coincidence, or does your company have more to do with Santa Claus than you are letting on? After all, your company is North Pole Enterprises, LLC and Santa Claus is known to inhabit the North Pole, and you admit that your company uses Naughty and Nice lists, just like Santa Claus. I have to ask this question: Are you sure you don't work for Santa Claus?"

"Objection," Peabody said, "this case is not about whether Mr. Snow works for Santa Claus."

Judge Stark was troubled about the direction this line of questioning was headed and asked Raker for an explanation.

"Your honor," Raker said, "it is clear that the prosecution, by putting on the testimony of Ms. Robertson, thinks my client is crazy, and therefore, cannot be trusted to tell the truth, simply because he believes he works for Santa Claus. I am entitled to explore with this witness whether he believes he works for Santa Claus."

Judge Stark said, “But you didn’t ask him whether he believes he works for Santa Claus; you asked him whether he does work for Santa Claus. There is a difference.”

“That is correct, your honor, because we intend to prove that he does.”

“That he does what?” Judge Stark asked.

“Work for Santa Claus, of course,” Raker said. With that, the audience erupted, causing Judge Stark to bang his gavel six times on the bench to restore order. During the ensuing chaos, Raker looked around, and for the first time, noticed the little girl with the pointy ears in the back of the courtroom; she was nodding approvingly in his direction.

Over the elevated voices in the courtroom, Judge Stark ordered the attorneys to approach the bench, and looked from one and to the other.

“Gentlemen,” he said, with an edge to his voice, “I had my doubts about this case from the very beginning, but now the two of you have taken those doubts to new heights. Mr. Peabody, you never should have put into evidence that the defendant believed himself to be Santa’s helper. You didn’t need to do it and look where it has gotten us. But at this point, as much as I would like to, I can’t turn back the clock. I have to give the defendant the right to ask questions about Santa Claus, no matter how harebrained the defense strategy may be. So, I am going to let this thing play out, but if either of you end up wasting the Court's time with too many visions of sugar plums dancing in the aisle, I swear, I will put you up on ethics charges with the State bar."

Meanwhile, Austin Land was busy sending another tweet, saying:

> **Austin Land** @ALandReporter Dec. 24
> Defense intends to prove Santa Claus is real. #courtroom3150

In the People's Court, there was electricity in the air.

When the audience had calmed down, Judge Stark instructed Raker to continue his cross-examination.

"Mr. Snow," Raker said, "let's go about this a little differently."

Snow said nothing.

Raker asked to approach the witness, and when permission was granted, he picked up his laptop and carried it with him. He then placed it on the ledge in front of the witness, opened its lid, and spun it around so Snow could read the screen. Then he retrieved the flash drive from the clerk and plugged it into the USB drive.

"Mr. Snow," Raker said, "since your company owns the flash drive, as you claim, I presume you have the passwords. Am I right?"

Snow said nothing; he simply typed something on the keyboard and waited for the next question.

"Let's start with the property database. Please describe for the Court what you see when you access that database," Raker instructed.

Snow opened the file, and briefly explained. "The property database contains the logistical information needed by the company to make deliveries to homes in this county."

Raker came around to Snow's side, and peeked over his shoulder, saying, "Isn't there more information than just the addresses to make deliveries?" Raker asked.

"Yes," Snow said. "We gather details about every property, because sometimes the toys children want are just too large. For example, a child may want a ping pong table, but there is no way to accommodate it in the home. This is a service we provide to parents, helping them know in advance whether their orders will fit their available space."

"Very well," Raker said, "but that doesn't explain this column right here." He pointed to the screen. Snow looked at it and said nothing.

"You don't have an answer, do you?" Raker asked, a mocking tone to his voice. "In any event, tell the Court what this column records."

"It lists, or records as you say, whether the home has any chimneys and if so, the number and locations of the chimneys."

"Go on," Raker prompted.

"If the home has no chimney, there is a picture of a door, with a letter 'F', 'B' or 'S' beside it. And if the home does have a chimney—"

"There is a check mark in the column, with a drop-down link for more information," Raker added, helpfully.

"Correct," Snow said.

"And when you hit the drop-down link on the home that has a chimney, what do you find?" Raker asked.

Snow tapped the keys. "What you find is a description of where the chimneys are located in the home, and other pertinent information, such as whether they are functioning or have been closed off."

"And what do the initials 'BA' mean beside one of the chimneys listed if there is more than one chimney in a home?" Raker asked.

Snow didn't like where this question was headed, but he responded. "Best available."

There was a low murmur among the audience.

"Mr. Snow," Raker said, moving to another topic, "let's talk now about the evaluation database on the flash drive. I presume you can access it as well."

Snow said nothing but his fingers flew across the keyboard on the computer, typing in another password. When he was done, he looked up at Raker.

"Tell the Court what you see at the top of the first page," Raker instructed.

"You can read it as well as I," Snow replied tersely, which didn't sit well with Judge Stark.

"Mr. Snow," Judge Stark said, "you came in here and volunteered to offer evidence and now that you have, you must abide by the rules of the Court, which include answering questions on cross-examination. Answer the question!"

Snow shifted on top of his stack of crossword books. "The title is 'Naughty and Nice Lists, Zone 1028, District 26, Collector First Class Henry Edmonds.'"

"And what version is this?" Raker asked.

Snow said nothing.

"I see that you are tongue-tied, Mr. Snow, so let me help you out. It says it is version 4.2. Was there a different version last year, say version 3.0?" Raker asked.

Again, Snow said nothing.

"Mr. Snow," Judge Stark leaned toward the witness, "I have no idea where Mr. Raker is headed with this line of questioning, but you need to answer the question."

"I can't."

"You can't, or you won't?" Judge Stark asked.

"I am bound by a confidentiality agreement not to disclose that information. It is a trade secret and I will lose my job if I say more. I won't do it."

There was silence in the courtroom, as everyone, including Judge Stark, pondered the significance of this turn of events. Here was a witness who claimed to work for a company that owned the flash drive, and who had the passwords to access its contents, but he was now refusing to cooperate regarding information related to the Naughty and Nice lists. Judge Stark knew that this would fuel the fire for those who wanted to believe that Henry Edmonds really did work for Santa Claus, but there was not much he could do. He could either let it pass or hold the man in contempt. Holding him in contempt would draw more attention to the issue, so he let it pass, and he hoped Raker would, too.

To Judge Stark's surprise, Raker did let it pass.

Raker had been thinking about the events at the Tipsy Tavern. He knew that Edmonds never saw Snow that night, and if Edmonds didn't have a clear view of Snow, perhaps Snow didn't have a clear view of Edmonds. One thing was for sure, Raker didn't trust Snow. Cross-examination was not the time to guess, but Raker felt he had little choice.

"Mr. Snow, you say you were a witness to an assault by my client, is that correct?" Raker asked.

"That is correct."

"You followed my client to the Tipsy Tavern and when you got there, you kept yourself hidden from his view, correct?" Raker asked.

"Yes," Snow replied.

"And, given your desire to stay concealed, you were not too close to him, correct?

"True. I was across the room, but I could definitely see him," Snow said.

"Could you hear him?" Raker asked.

"No, I wasn't that close," Snow answered.

"And were you standing or seated at the time?"

"I was standing in the corner, directly across the room from him."

After accepting the case, Raker had stopped by the tavern to investigate, and as he and Snow were going back and forth, he processed the details of what he had seen. He considered the angles of the room, where furniture was located, and the impediments, if any, that could have blocked Snow's view. Then he smiled to himself.

"And what was between you and the assault you say you witnessed?"

"Not much other than a pool table, and some people playing pool."

Raker paused, making the witness and everyone in the room wonder if he was stumped, and he asked: "How tall are you, Mr. Snow?"

Snow didn't respond.

"I don't mean to be demeaning, Mr. Snow," Raker said, "nor am I making fun of your height; your height just happens to be a fact in the case, so I will ask you again; how tall are you?"

"Three feet tall," Snow said.

"That is not quite as tall as the top of the pool table, correct?" Raker asked.

Snow paused.

"Take your time," Raker offered.

"That is about right," Snow said.

"So let me get this straight," Raker said, "in order to see this alleged assault, you could not have been standing, because if you were, you would have been looking directly into the side of the pool table, correct?"

"OK, I was on my knees, but I could see them." Snow was not backing down.

"But unless you had X-ray vision, Mr. Snow, the most you could see were the shoes, ankles, calves and maybe the knees of Mr. Edmonds and Ms. Robertson, true?"

Again, Snow didn't respond right away, and Raker pressed ahead.

"Isn't the reason you knew that Ms. Robertson fell and hit her head," Raker asked, "because you were on your knees, looking under the pool table, when you saw her head hit the floor?"

"He pushed her, and I know it," Snow said.

"And yet, you did not see him do so, did you?" Raker looked right at the judge as he asked the question.

"Answer the question, Mr. Snow." Judge Stark was tiring of this witness.

"I did not see him push her down, but I know he did it." Snow said.

Raker turned to Judge Stark. "Your honor, we move to strike the speculative portion of Mr. Snow's response. It is clear that he did not see my client push Ms. Robertson."

"Sustained," Judge Stark said. "I will not consider his speculation and his admission is noted for the record. Is there anything else, Mr. Raker?"

Raker had just a few more questions.

"Mr. Snow," Raker began, "with respect to the codes 'F','B' and 'S' used in the property database, is it true that the letter 'F' means front door, the letter 'B' means back door and the letter 'S' means side door?"

"You are correct, counselor."

"Is it also true that these codes are used only for homes with no chimney?"

"That is true," Snow said.

"To summarize," Raker said, "you work for a company that does the same kind of work as Santa Claus, whose delivery schedule and fiscal year are the same as that of Santa Claus, and yet, you claim not to be affiliated with Santa Claus in any way.

"You also work in security for an organization seeking to recover perhaps the most important lists to your business this time of year, the Naughty and Nice lists, which happen to be just as important to Santa Claus, and yet, you claim not to be affiliated with Santa Claus in any way.

"You also collect information on homes, in order to deliver presents by December 25th, and one of the key pieces of data you collect is information about chimneys and alternative access points if there is no chimney, and yet, you claim not to be affiliated with Santa Claus in any way.

"And, finally, when I ask you questions about the change from version 3.0 to version 4.2, you shut down and refuse to answer my questions. Did I sum matters up accurately, Mr. Snow?"

Snow didn't respond.

"The fact is," Raker said, "you haven't told this Court the truth, the whole truth and nothing but the truth, have you, Mr. Snow?"

"I have told you what I am permitted to tell you, counselor, and now that you have twisted my words beyond reality, I must be off, because, believe it or not, some of us have to work on Christmas. But before I go, remember this," speaking as much to the audience as to Raker, "I tried to save Christmas for the children of this community, but without that flash drive, it won't happen." Snow began to shift to rise from his chair.

"I am not through yet, Mr. Snow," Raker said. "You say the flash drive and all the information on it belongs to your company; is that right?"

"Correct."

"Then, please open the database on the flash

drive, previously described to this Court as The Archives."

"Well done, counselor. You have guessed correctly that I don't hold the password to that database, and I suspect you will use this information to convince the Court that my company cannot possibly be the rightful owner of the flash drive or the information on it. If that happens, it will be another example of lawyers making people unhappy, because when Christmas doesn't come, it will be your fault and the fault of your client. May I go now?"

"You may," Raker said, and with that, Snow stepped down, walked across the courtroom and out the courtroom door.

The audience began to whisper. At first, it sounded like the muffled chatter of telephone operators behind a technical-support person in a distant call center. Then, as the questions and speculative answers began to flow back and forth among the spectators, the sound became more like noise, and the courtroom got louder. The cause for this noise was the excellent lawyering of Thad Raker. The audience believed he had made a good case for reasonable doubt.

Judge Stark took control, and the room quieted. "Mr. Peabody, do you have any more witnesses?"

Peabody said again, as he had the day before, that he wanted to call defendant Henry Edmonds as a witness. Before Judge Stark could deny the request for the second time on Fifth Amendment grounds, Raker informed the Court that his client would answer Mr. Peabody's questions.

"Fine," Judge Stark said, throwing up his hands, thinking that this was another unusual development in a particularly unusual case. "Let's take his testimony after our morning recess."

As the courtroom came alive with sounds of informality, Austin Land picked up his smartphone, and tapped his latest tweet, saying:

> **Austin Land** @ALandReporter Dec. 24
> Santa's helper will testify to take on the prosecution!
> #courtroom3150

11:15 a.m.

When Judge Stark re-entered the courtroom, the spectator pews were more crowded than before, with more and more people squeezing in to find out what would happen to the friendly-looking old man named Henry Edmonds. In front of the courthouse, two local TV stations had positioned trucks with large antennas, so they could broadcast live the events as they unfolded. To top it off, it had begun to snow.

Edmonds had already taken his place in the witness chair. He was ready to proceed, as were Peabody and Raker.

Judge Stark tapped his gavel on his bench and made a few comments. He reminded the audience of the need to remain quiet during testimony and added that the trial might have to proceed through the lunch break, because of a heavy snowstorm predicted to hit the area. If anyone wanted to leave, he said, they should do it now. No one moved.

"Proceed, Mr. Peabody," Judge Stark said.

"Thank you, your honor." Peabody turned toward the witness and said, "Good morning, Mr. Edmonds."

"Good morning, sir."

"I would like to start off with a few questions that have been nagging at me since the beginning of this case."

"I will do what I can to help," Edmonds said.

"Do you believe in Santa Claus?" Peabody asked.

"Of course, I do," Edmonds said. "He is the spirit of Christmas giving."

"I don't mean in spirit, sir," Peabody was a little annoyed at Edmonds' play on words. "I mean, do you actually believe that there is a living, breathing Santa Claus?"

At that, a sense of nervousness spread through the courtroom. Elizabeth Foley, for one, was particularly worried about her second-grade students. She didn't want a negative answer to Peabody's question to leave them in tears, nor did she want to be blamed by their parents for spoiling that magical time in life when children believe in Santa Claus.

The parents who were there with their children were equally nervous, thinking how they might explain an answer that Santa Claus is not real.

Kay Stark was on edge because she knew how much it would trouble her husband to have his long career on the bench end in a joke, how he would regret being labeled as the judge who stole Christmas.

"I remind you that you are under oath, Mr. Edmonds," Peabody said. "Please answer the question."

Edmonds did not answer right away. Until this moment, his thoughts had been clouded by fear and anxiety. He had been afraid he would not be able to continue doing the job he loved and worried about the children if their Christmas did not arrive. But he realized he was not alone; he had help, a good friend seated in the first row on his side of the courtroom. The little girl with elfin ears smiled at him. He smiled back. He was at peace with what he was doing. He knew his method for righting the wrong was ill-conceived, but his heart was in the right place. He concluded that there was no time for looking back and he vowed to himself to focus and to maintain his composure. He wanted to save Christmas. He figured now was as good a time as any to start.

"Mr. Peabody, I know that I am under oath, but I understand that you are an officer of the Court, bound to be honest, without the requirement of an oath, so I ask you a question, similar to but a little different than the one you asked me. Did you ever believe in Santa Claus?"

Peabody looked around the room before he responded. He saw the children who looked at him with large, hopeful eyes. He saw Judy Robertson watching him with concern on her face. He said, "The rules of court do not require me to answer your question, Mr. Edmonds, but I will do so anyway. Of course I believed in the existence of Santa Claus!"

"Are you a sane person, Mr. Peabody?" Edmonds asked

"If I were insane, do you think I would know?" Peabody replied. "But yes, I believe myself to be a sane person."

"And you passed the mental fitness examination to be licensed as a lawyer, did you not?" Edmonds asked.

"I did, but I am the one who is supposed to be asking the questions, Mr. Edmonds." Peabody glanced at Judge Stark but received no help.

"One last question," Edmonds said. "Do you believe that a person who believes in Santa Claus can be an honest person?"

Peabody saw the trap, and, unfortunately for him, he saw no way out.

After Peabody was forced to acknowledge that honest people can believe in Santa Claus, Edmonds made it clear that he was one of those believers. He believed in Santa Claus, he told the Court, and he was ready to tell the truth about what happened at the tavern, what happened with the flash drive and what needed to happen to save Christmas.

"Let's start with the Tipsy Tavern," Peabody said, hoping to get back to the facts. "Do you admit grabbing Ms. Robertson by the arms?"

"I do," Edmonds said.

"And after that, you threw her down, correct?"

"No I did not. She tried to pull away, I let loose of her arms and she tripped and fell," Edmonds said.

"Why did you grab her by the arms in the first place?"

"Because she was trying to take the flash drive from my pocket."

"So you are calling Ms. Robertson, a well-respected member of this community, a person who helps the poor, a liar?" Peabody asked.

"No, I am not," Edmonds replied. "She is a good person; she is not a liar. She was just confused and her judgment was clouded. I would never try to hurt her."

"OK," Peabody asked, "but tell me this, did you wrongfully enter the county office building, break into the safe of the director of revaluation, and take the flash drive that is Exhibit 1 in this case?"

"I simply took back what belonged to my boss," Edmonds said. "There was nothing wrongful about it. You should ask Ms. Robertson; she had never seen the flash drive before I showed it to her, and she had no idea then and has no idea now, how we collect the information on it."

"But how did you do it? How did you get it back?" Peabody asked. "The county office building has an alarm system, with patrol guards, and the safe has a nine-digit combination. You don't look like a safe-cracker to me."

"You need answers, I know," Edmonds said, "but sometimes, answers are not really necessary in this world, and just because you don't understand how something happens does not mean it is impossible to do."

"Kind of like magic, huh," Peabody was dismissive.

"Now that is a good way to put it, Mr. Peabody; yes, it is kind of like magic," Edmonds said.

"OK, if you won't explain how you got the device back, then explain why you gave it to her in the first place." Peabody said.

"I would be glad to," Edmonds said. "I gave it to her because she is a good, smart, talented person who could solve the problem, and because I know a secret from her past that made me think she would be more than willing to help. Unfortunately, I misjudged the situation. Her emotional wounds were deeper than I thought and when faced with the reality of the current situation, she overreacted."

"Continue," Peabody said. He didn't want to be fascinated by this old man's storytelling, but he felt himself slip. The silence from the spectators behind him revealed that they were spellbound.

"Ms. Robertson cares for people. She always has cared, but she has not always been 'Ms.' Robertson. Like all the adults in this room, she once was a child, and like you, Mr. Peabody, and like the other adults in this room, she once believed in Santa Claus.

"But there comes a time in every child's life when doubts creep in, causing them to question and eventually abandon their beliefs. For some, it happens over time. For others, it is abrupt, and when that happens, it is hard to get over. We call it PTNBS, or Post-Traumatic Non-Belief Syndrome. Some cases are worse than others and can last for years. The cause of the trauma can be buried, only to surface years later. I believe that happened to Judy Robertson. She had a reaction upon seeing the information on the flash drive and, as I said before, she overreacted."

"We will come back to that in a moment." Peabody snapped himself back to business. "Let's walk through the timeline first."

Edmonds confirmed the sequence of events, starting with his meeting with Robertson at the Salvation Army orientation session. From that first meeting, until the time the flash drive was retaken by Edmonds, the testimony of Edmonds and Robertson matched up. Edmonds had given her the flash drive and had allowed her to copy what was on the property database for use in her work for the county. He also had asked for her help with respect to the evaluation database.

"What was she supposed to do with the evaluation database?" Peabody asked.

"I needed her expertise as a computer programmer to revert the Naughty and Nice computer program from version 4.2 back to version 3.0. As you know, Mr. Snow was reluctant to answer questions about these two versions, and ..." Edmonds paused to look at the faces in the courtroom. "... and I understand his reluctance, because sometimes, too much information can lead to as much disappointment as not enough information.

"Anyway, I can tell you that Mr. Snow and I work for the same organization. Unlike him, I don't know the legal details of how the operation is set up, but I know that it has been around for a long time, and I know that we exist to do good work. Our mission statement from the beginning has been to make children happy, but as we have gotten more technological in our operations, I fear that we have lost sight of that goal. Version 4.2 is one of those aberrations."

"Explain," Peabody said.

"It's like this," Edmonds said. "We used to collect the information in the field and then compile one list of all the Naughty and Nice children on a very long scroll, which allowed us to make orderly, subjective decisions. True, this did require us to check the list twice, at each level of our operations, right up to Santa Claus himself, but that was a small price to pay in order to maintain the personal touch in the decision-making process. With the use of technology, however, that changed. Programs were developed to help decide who was Naughty and who was Nice, and the machines took over.

"We became forced to label a child Naughty if the computer said so, regardless of any mitigating factors, which is much like the potential inequity criminal defendants face with minimum-sentencing guidelines. It removes all discretion from the judge making the decision." Edmonds looked toward Judge Stark.

Judge Stark seemed to nod, just slightly, as if he agreed with Edmonds.

"Anyway," Edmonds said, "to make matters worse, someone came up with a computer program designed to determine, unequivocally, who is Naughty and who is Nice."

"So how did it work, and why did you need Ms. Robertson's help?" Peabody asked.

"The computer geeks in our IT department developed two lists, columns in the database, and a series of categories to be considered by the computer program to determine who went on which list, such as politeness, kindness, helpfulness and so forth. Success in each category was to be measured on a scale of 1 to 5, with 5 being the best and 1 being the worst. Ten categories were created to evaluate each child throughout the year. How it was done is something of a trade secret, but at the end of the year, we had fairly reliable scores in ten categories. We took those scores, or I should say, the computer took those scores and averaged them. In version 3.0, children who scored at least a 3 were classified Nice. A score less than 3 put them in the Naughty category. This system has been in place for ten years, and for the most part, it has resulted in tallies similar to the scores under the old paper system. Despite my initial reservations with the technology, the computerized rating system seemed to be working, but then things changed this year. That change is why I needed Ms. Robertson's help."

"Go on," Peabody said.

"The new software, Version 4.2, was a serious change that would have terrible repercussions. I needed someone with Ms. Robertson's talents to help me. I have kept tabs on her over the years, you see."

"What do you mean by 'keeping tabs on her'?" Peabody asked.

"I followed her career. I have done it for years with all the children; I like to see how they turn out after they stop believing."

"And what did you mean by 'terrible repercussions'?" Peabody asked.

"Version 4.2 changed the ranking system, simple as that. In order to be considered Nice under this new version, a child has to get an overall average score of 4.2. Anything less puts them on the Naughty list. It means that a child who is good, or even very good, is still not Nice, for purposes of our ranking system." His voice rose now and he clinched his fists. "They forgot the very purpose of the organization for which they work. I wanted to fix that, and went to Ms. Robertson for help. I was hoping she could come up with a way to change the ranking system in the program, without alerting my superiors."

"So why did you take it back, the flash drive, that is?" Peabody asked.

"I started getting alerts on the mobile device that all collectors are required to carry," Edmonds explained. "It helps us keep track of real time updates to the lists, child by child, throughout the year. The final tabulation in December leads to the final determination of Naughty or Nice, but the constant updates help us monitor the children more closely. Historically, children start out on the Naughty side of the ledger at the beginning of the year and as they get closer to Christmas, their rankings improve, causing them to flip from Naughty to Nice. Every now and then, however, but not often, the rankings on children flip late in the year in the other direction, from Nice to Naughty."

"And how is that relevant in this case?" Peabody asked.

"On the second day Ms. Robertson had the flash drive in her possession," Edmonds answered, "my mobile device starting pinging every thirty seconds and what I saw startled me, because every one of the pings alerted me that another child in my area of responsibility had flipped from Nice to Naughty. Within twelve hours, more than fourteen hundred children had been added to the Naughty list, all of whom had never been there before, and the changes kept coming. I could only conclude that Ms. Robertson was responsible for these changes, so I had to get the flash drive back."

"And what motive would she have to do that?" Peabody asked.

"I have a theory," Edmonds said, "but I hope I am wrong. My theory is that it relates back to the last Christmas she was a believer. You remember, Mr. Peabody, because you were there for her."

This caught Peabody off-guard. How could Edmonds know about his past with Robertson?

"You will have to be more specific," Peabody said to Edmonds, bracing himself as he spoke.

"Ms. Robertson was the victim of a mistake in my organization, a mistake that she has not forgotten or forgiven to this day. No system is perfect, and we rarely make mistakes, but on this particular Christmas, we were still passing the local Naughty and Nice lists up the chain of command, using paper for recording purposes. The transport at the time was by carrier pigeon, which was deemed the safest and quickest way to get all the lists to our headquarters up North. That year, I completed my work, wrapped the list for my area tightly in a protective cover and sent it on its way. When the pigeon left me on December 1st, Judy Robertson was on my Nice list, and a very nice girl she had been for the whole year. If we had used computer rankings at the time, she would have ranked well above 4.5 on a 5.0 scale. When she woke up on Christmas morning, however, she was shocked to learn that she had no presents from Santa Claus, because the official record said she was Naughty.

"It took me years to figure out what happened. The pigeon carrying the list was blown off course by a major storm and had to bed down in the snow before it could fly on. Unfortunately, the snow penetrated the outer protective shell of the list and smudged some of the entries, causing her entry to be misunderstood, and the rest is history. That was the Christmas that Judy Robertson stopped believing."

The spectators were listening to Henry Edmonds but they were looking at Judy Robertson, who sat behind Peabody, hands folded in her lap, her eyes cast down. Those in the courtroom who supported Edmonds were suspicious of Robertson's motives for the flash drive, but they were becoming more sympathetic to her as a person. She had once been a good little girl who believed in Santa Claus, and Santa let her down. The children in the courtroom thought that especially unfair.

Edmonds continued: "Thinking she was to blame for the coal in her stocking, Judy lived her life trying to do right by others. It was her caring spirit that caused me to reach out to her, and I thought she would help me, because she of all people could empathize with children being wrongly classified as Naughty, but she must have snapped. Maybe it was PTNBS, because I don't really think she wanted to hurt the children. Maybe she was so traumatized that she wanted to hurt the organization that hurt her, figuring that classification mistakes on a massive scale would bring the organization to its knees. Children everywhere would stop believing, and Christmas as we know it, would come to an end."

"And you think that a person as giving as Ms. Robertson could do this?" Peabody asked.

"She is a very giving person," Edmonds nodded, "but apparently, she is a person who is not very forgiving."

Peabody's posture suddenly changed. He stood slightly, placed both hands on the table in front of him and leaned his upper body forward. Anger showed in his face, and Peabody eyed Edmonds like a cat eyes its prey. He continued with his questioning, but this time, he used a sharp, lecturing tone.

"So you come in here," Peabody said, "and you blame Ms. Robertson, after all she has done for this community, with absolutely no proof of any kind that she is at fault for the flash drive problem you describe."

Edmonds opened his mouth to speak but Peabody didn't break stride. "Did it occur to you, Mr. Edmonds, that the mere fact you believe yourself to be innocent does not mean that Ms. Robertson is guilty?"

"I see your point," Edmonds said, "but—"

"No 'buts,' Mr. Edmonds," Peabody said, interrupting Edmonds' attempt to explain himself. "You have admitted that Ms. Robertson could have been mistaken about the assault charge, but is that any reason to say in open court that she tampered with the flash drive?"

Edmonds started to answer, but Peabody interrupted his effort. "Did it occur to you that someone else might be responsible for the flash drive problem, perhaps someone with more knowledge than Ms. Robertson about how the computer program works?"

"I don't know," Edmonds admitted. "That never occurred to me."

"In fact, you never asked her what happened with the evaluation database, did you, because you assumed that she was the culprit, correct?" Peabody didn't hide his anger.

Edmonds paused. He looked at Judy Robertson, who looked shaken. Then he looked at his attorney, who was unable to offer any help. Had he made a mistake? Was Judy Robertson once again a victim of a terrible misunderstanding? If so, he thought, he needed to make things right, and without delay.

"Mr. Peabody," Edmonds said, "I take your point. Perhaps I did jump to conclusions. Maybe Judy Robertson is a victim, once again, and maybe there is another explanation for the problem with the flash drive. If so, I am very, very sorry for suggesting she is at fault."

"One more question, Mr. Edmonds," Peabody said. "Do you have the password to The Archives section of the flash drive?"

Edmonds was quiet for a moment, and then said, "No, I do not."

"How then," Peabody asked, "do you expect this Court to believe that you are the rightful owner of the information on Exhibit 1 if you don't know how to gain access to the information?"

"I can't answer that question," Edmonds said, "but I can tell you that unless I can get that flash drive back today, fix it, and get it in the right hands, Mr. Snow will be right. Christmas will not come to this community."

"And I suppose after the tales you have spun and the unproven accusations you have made, you still want this Court to take your word for it?"

As quickly as he finished speaking, Peabody said to Judge Stark, "Your honor, we withdraw that question. We are done with this witness."

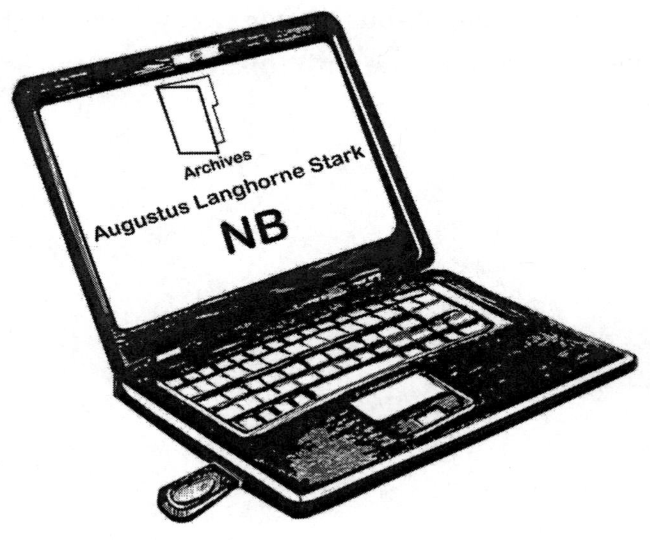

12:15 p.m.

After Edmonds had finished testifying, Judge Stark had ordered a break and told the lawyers to approach the bench.

"Gentlemen," he said, when they approached, "it is time that we had a little talk in my chambers. Raker, you are not required to bring your client with you, but I recommend you do so. Whether he says anything is up to you and him. Bring your laptop, Raker, and Exhibit 1 with it. Peabody, bring Ms. Robertson." He left no option for Peabody to say no, and then he commanded, "Let's go!"

Austin Land watched as the lawyers fetched Edmonds and Robertson and left through the side door of the courtroom, following Judge Stark. Trials are supposed to occur in the open, and it appeared to Land that Judge Stark was pulling an end run on the public. Land couldn't let that happen, but before he got up, he sent another tweet:

> **Austin Land** @ALandReporter Dec. 24
> Mystery deepens as to who hacked the Naughty and Nice Lists. #courtroom3150

Judge Stark's office was about ten feet by twelve feet. Besides his chair, there were only two other chairs in his office, so he dragged two more chairs inside and told everyone to sit down as he shut the door behind him. When everyone was settled, he said, "I called you in here to—"

Just then, he was interrupted by a knock on the door. "We are busy," Judge Stark shouted, but the knock came again, so Judge Stark got up and went to the door, all patience gone. When he opened the door, he saw Austin Land, the local reporter, whom Judge Stark blamed for the publicity surrounding this case.

"What do you want?" Judge Stark grumbled.

"I want access to this proceeding, as public-access laws allow."

"Well, you are not welcome here." Judge Stark started to shut the door.

Land put his foot in the door to prevent it from closing. "Judge Stark, with all due respect, the public deserves access, and if I have to call the newspaper's lawyers, I will. I promise. This conference may be over before the lawyers can act, but the delay will not prevent me from writing about this secret meeting and it will not prevent my editorial board from chastising you for your actions."

"You want access, do you?" Retirement was looking better and better to Judge Stark. "Fine, you have access. Come in, stand over there, and keep your mouth shut!"

The lawyers looked suspiciously at Land, but said nothing.

"Now is everyone ready?" Judge Stark asked. It was a question not meant for a reply, just a prelude for the uncertainty to come. Then the tirade began.

"Does anyone know how long I have been a judge?" Judge Stark asked. Peabody started to speak, but Judge Stark held up his hand, stopping him. "Thirty-five years. And does anyone know the name of the worst case, ever, that I have been required to handle as a judge?"

No one spoke. They knew better.

"The State v. Henry Edmonds." Turning to Land, he said, "you can quote me on that, Newspaper Man, because I am retiring soon, and the truth is the truth!"

"Your honor… " Peabody began.

"Shut up, Peabody. You are the reason I am having such a good time this Christmas Eve. If it hadn't been for you bringing this case to trial, we wouldn't have a packed courtroom full of children waiting on me to put one of Santa's helpers in jail, and wondering whether the Naughty and Nice lists will be fixed in time for Christmas."

"And as for you, Raker." The judge turned on the defense attorney. "You should have struck a plea bargain on Day One, and your failure to do so has put your client in jeopardy of spending time in jail at Christmas and the loss of the flash drive."

No one spoke. Land took notes, but didn't look up, for fear of catching the gaze of Judge Stark. Judy Robertson had her hands in her lap, a sad look on her face. Henry Edmonds looked equally dismayed, but not for fear of spending time in jail. What concerned him most was the fact that time was running out. Christmas was less than twelve hours away.

"Before we go any further," Judge Stark said, "I need more information about this flash drive."

He looked at Raker, and asked him whether his client was willing to talk.

"What he says can and will be held against him," Judge Stark said, "but the quickest way to get to the truth in this case is for me to ask my own questions."

Edmonds looked at Raker, and then nodded yes, he would cooperate.

Judge Stark turned to Peabody. "I know Ms. Robertson has already testified, and that some of her testimony has been called into question by other witnesses. Perjury is still on the table for her, and what she says can and will be held against her, too, but she can add to this discussion, if she is so inclined," Judge Stark said.

Like Edmonds, Robertson gave her consent to participate.

"Good," Judge Stark said. Looking hard at Edmonds, he said, "I have enough evidence to rule on the assault charge." Turning to Raker he said, "Open that computer of yours and let's talk about these databases."

Raker opened the computer, and waited for his next instructions.

"You don't have to open the property database, because I have enough information about it," Judge

Stark said, "although it is not clear to me why anyone would need detailed information on chimney access points, unless, of course, he is a jolly old elf driving a sleigh led by eight tiny reindeer."

There was silence in the room as Judge Stark looked around, daring anyone to comment.

"Now, Raker," Judge Stark said, "let's get that evaluation database open."

Raker placed the laptop in front of Edmonds, who typed in the password for the evaluation database, and Raker found himself staring at the first page of the Naughty and Nice Lists, Version 4.2.

Judge Stark then told his audience that they were not there to solve the mysteries of Christmas, nor was this trial going to be a referendum on the existence of Santa Claus. He described what he had heard about the lists as very entertaining, but not very convincing. His concerns were legal ownership of the database information and whether or not a crime had been committed in his jurisdiction to corrupt the information.

"Ms. Robertson," he asked, "were you able to open this database when you had it in you possession and, if you did so, did it look anything like what it does now?"

Robertson leaned in to look over Raker's shoulder at the computer screen. She recognized the title, the version, and the two columns, or lists, but there was one glaring difference. She swallowed hard, and said, "Judge Stark, when I accessed this database, at least eighty percent of the children on the first page were in the Nice column. As I look at it now, they are all classified Naughty."

With that, Edmonds leaned in close to Raker, put his finger on the up/down curser and started scrolling through the pages. Name after name after name were classified Naughty. He grabbed the laptop off Raker's lap and did a quick search for all names on the Nice list and to his surprise, no names appeared. None. Confused, he continued to tap away at the keyboard, but this time, he was searching for all names listed on the Naughty list, and when the search results came in, he slumped back in his chair.

To his utter disbelief, there were 85,424 names on the Naughty list, which just happened to be the same number of believing children who lived in the county.

"What did you do?" Edmonds turned to Robertson. "And why did you do it?"

"I didn't mean to do this." She was trembling. Peabody reached over to comfort her, but there was little he could do. She buried her face in her hands and sobbed.

A minute later, while Robertson was trying to gather herself, Judge Stark asked Edmonds a question. "Would Mr. Snow have any reason to want to tamper with this database?"

Edmonds thought for a moment and said, "I can't believe he would intentionally sabotage the Naughty and Nice lists. It is true that he was the driving force behind the development of Version 4.2, but even under that version, the list classifies some children as Nice."

By this time, Robertson had regained control of her emotions and was sitting quietly, thinking about all the good children who would go without Christmas this year, and that it was her fault. Until this moment, some thirty years after she was snubbed on Christmas Day, she had not believed; she had lost faith in all things magical, including Santa Claus. But the events of the last month and four days had affected her deeply and she was beginning, just beginning, to believe again. Edmonds sensed it.

In a friendlier voice, Edmonds said to Robertson, "Maybe if you can tell us what happened, we can figure this out."

"What I said in court was true," Robertson replied. "When you told me you worked for Santa

Claus and you needed help with the Naughty and Nice lists, I thought you were crazy. I am not proud of misleading you, but I was concerned about the property information you had in your possession. For all I knew, you had stolen it from our office. When I got deeper into it, I noticed little things, like the chimney information, which didn't make sense to me. So I decided to look at the evaluation database, and it started me thinking. I wondered whether, even if this were a hoax, I could redesign the program to do what you wanted, set the lowest number for being rated as Nice at 3 rather than at 4.2. So I tried." Her voice trailed off. "I just failed."

"Tell us what happened," Judge Stark prompted.

"The first thing I did was study the system set up for the database and when I felt confident that I knew how it operated, I designed a program that should have worked. But when I implemented the new program, the database went into lockdown mode, with a ten-minute countdown timer. It was like a ticking bomb. I didn't know what to do. I tried every workaround possible, but the clock just kept on ticking, and finally, it struck zero and the screen went blank. I was tired and confused, so I put the flash drive in the safe with every intention of trying to solve the problem the next day. Only the next day came, and the flash drive was gone."

"I suppose that leads us to the Tipsy Tavern," Judge Stark said.

"Yes, sir," Robertson said. "I wanted to get the flash drive back so I could try to fix the mess I created, but Mr. Edmonds misunderstood my intentions. He was trying to protect the flash drive. I suppose if I had been in his position, I would have done the same."

"But what about the assault charge?" Judge Stark asked.

"Did he push me, or did I fall, that is the question," Robertson said. "I don't want him to go to jail. Not given what is at stake."

"Protecting the flash drive, even if it belonged to him, is no excuse for assaulting a woman," Judge Stark said.

"But if he goes to jail, there is no way we can save Christmas."

"So now you want to work with your alleged assailant?"

"Yes, sir," Robertson said, looking at Edmonds, who smiled at her.

"And I suppose that in order to save Christmas, the two of you need the flash drive," Judge Stark said.

Edmonds and Robertson looked at each other, then back at Judge Stark, and said yes, at the same time.

"It can't happen," Judge Stark said, "for a number of reasons."

Hearing these words, Edmonds' mouth dropped open, and Robertson gasped. Peabody and Raker didn't know what to say. Land continued to take notes.

"First of all," Judge Stark said, "I don't believe the stories you folks have spun in my courtroom for the benefit of the gullible public. Mr. First Amendment here," pointing to Austin Land in the corner, "has certainly made a name for himself reporting on this case, but I doubt he believes any part of what he has written in the last 24 hours; to him, this case just sells papers.

"The first problem is that I don't know who owns the flash drive or the information on it. Mr. Snow made the best case for ownership of the device itself, with the bill of sale he produced in court, but he made a poor case for ownership of the information because he did not have the password to all the databases. For that matter," Judge Stark said, looking around the room, "neither does anyone else in this room.

"The second problem is that the flash drive is logged as evidence in this case, a case that should never have been brought in the first place. Even if I wanted to release the flash drive, my hands are tied at this point, because there is insufficient evidence before me to make it possible. Whoever wants it will have to file a separate civil lawsuit and bring forth convincing evidence of ownership."

Edmonds raised his hand, as if he were in class in grade school.

"What is it, Mr. Edmonds?" Judge Stark asked.

"Sir," Edmonds said, "you may not believe in my work, or the work of my boss ..."

"Spit it out," Judge Stark interrupted. "By 'boss', do you mean Santa Claus?"

"Yes, sir, I do" Edmonds said. "You may not believe, but there are lots of good children who do believe, and if we don't fix the lists in time, tomorrow will be the day when their belief in Santa Claus comes to an end."

"That is not my problem," Judge Stark said. "Again, you have given me no persuasive evidence to release the flash drive, and I mean absolutely none."

The room got quiet, as realization set in in that all was lost, that Christmas was not going to come for thousands of good and truly Nice children.

And then the silence was broken by a small voice from atop the credenza to the side of Judge Stark's desk.

"Would it help," the voice asked, "if you could see the evidence?"

Everyone in the room turned at once to look in the direction of the voice, and what they saw was a cute little girl with pointy ears sitting on the credenza, her knees pulled up to her chest, and her arms wrapped around them. She was swaying forward and backward and had a mischievous smile on her face.

"What is your name, little girl?" Judge Stark asked, "And how did you get in here?"

"My name is not important," she said, "and as for how I came in here, I arrived while everyone was arguing. You were all too busy to notice."

"You have some evidence?" Judge Stark asked.

"Yes, I do, kind sir" she said, "but before I provide it, you may need a little more background information. By now, you know that Judy and Henry are not bad people. He didn't assault her any more than she meant to damage the flash drive. What you don't know is why the flash drive was damaged or who owns the information on it, and that is why you are reluctant to release it."

She paused for a moment to look around the room, then continued: "Each one of you has played or will play a vital role in making this a special

Christmas for many children, but you will need to be creative.

"First," she said, "let's talk about the reason the flash drive went into lockdown mode when Judy tried to help. Version 4.2 has a special security system designed to avoid tampering, but I have learned that the security protocol is defective. When Judy implemented her new program, in override mode, it did work, but only to a point. When the first child was changed to Nice under the program she developed, the system shut down and began to change all the Nice classifications to Naughty."

"So what you are saying," Robertson asked, "is that it was the defective security system, not my program that caused the classifications to be changed for all the children?"

"Correct," the little girl said.

Relief showed on Robertson's face. "With that information, I think I know how to fix the problem," Robertson said to Edmonds.

"Aren't we forgetting something here?" Judge Stark asked. "You can't fix anything on the flash drive, because you can't have it. I am bound by law to hold it."

Again, the voice from atop the credenza piped in. "But, kind sir, that is only true if you don't have the evidence, and I have the evidence you need." And with that, she jumped down, and skipped the short distance across the room to where Raker was sitting with the laptop.

"May I?" she asked, holding out her hands.

"By all means," Raker said, glad to be rid of the responsibility.

The little girl hopped up on Judge Stark's desk and typed away on the laptop until she had what she wanted. Flipping the screen around for Judge Stark to see, she said, "I give you The Archives."

Judge Stark was puzzled. "But I thought nobody had the password to this database."

"Nobody who testified in court," she said, "but I have always had it. In fact, I am one of the keepers of The Archives, a responsibility I take very seriously."

"Let me guess," Judge Stark said, "you work for Mr. Edmonds' boss, too."

"You are a very smart man, kind sir" she replied, "and you are absolutely right. I am an elf and I work for Santa Claus."

Austin Land stopped taking notes and looked at her. The girl had been appearing and disappearing for the last twenty-four hours, and she had the password that had eluded all the witnesses in the case. He could not make sense of it.

The lawyers and Judge Stark were dumbstruck. Robertson was smiling, with tears of joy in her eyes. Edmonds was looking on in admiration for his brave little friend. She could be in a lot of trouble, even more than he, for telling these secrets.

"And you just expect me to believe you are an elf, that you work for Santa Claus and that the flash drive should be released to Mr. Edmonds?" Judge Stark asked.

"Oh, no," the little girl said, "if that were the case, I wouldn't have opened The Archives and I wouldn't be showing you what I am about to show you. The fact is," she continued, "you lawyers are the most doubting humans alive. You wallow in rules of evidence and burdens of proof. You can't take anything at face value. We have to use more extreme measures on folks like you."

Judge Stark couldn't believe what he was hearing. This little girl claiming to be an elf was lecturing him in a condescending manner in his own chambers. He had had enough.

"That's it," he said, rising from behind his desk, "this case is over. I am going back in my courtroom and announce my ruling."

"Nineteen fifty-three," said the little girl, looking at the computer screen, "you were eight years old,

Judge Stark, and that was the year it happened for you."

Judge Stark stopped in his tracks, and looked at the little girl. "What did you say?" he asked.

"It's right here, in The Archives," the little girl said. "The year was 1953. You were eight years old and you were having doubts about Santa Claus. You still wanted to believe, but some of your friends and your older brothers were making fun of you. That was the year you wanted a Red Ryder BB gun with the compass in the stock, just like the present made popular years later in the movie 'A Christmas Story'."

"Great movie," Land said.

"I told you to be quiet," Judge Stark barked.

The little girl continued. "Anyway, that is what you wanted, but you also wanted the respect of your friends and your older brothers, and that won out over your desire for the BB gun, so you told them that you did not believe in Santa Claus, and you told your parents, too. When Christmas day arrived, you secretly wanted to believe, because you wanted that BB gun, but you had made a public statement of non-belief, and that was that. Though a good kid, your actions shifted you into The Archives, with the notation NB, for Non-Believer."

"How could you possibly know any of that?" Judge Stark asked.

"How do reindeers fly?" she responded.

"I mean," Judge Stark said, "how could you know something that only I knew? I never told anyone, not even my parents, what I wanted that Christmas. It was a test to see whether Santa Claus was real."

"You never believed again, did you?" the little girl asked.

"No, I didn't," Judge Stark acknowledged.

"Kind sir, is everything you believe dependent upon what you can see and feel?" the little girl asked.

"I believe in God," Judge Stark answered, "so the obvious answer to your question is no; my religious beliefs are not subject to verification."

"Then why is it such a stretch for you to consider the possibility that Santa Claus is real?" she asked.

Before he could answer, she handed him the computer and said, "Here, take a look at your Christmas history. If it takes seeing for you to believe in Santa Claus, you will find that every single toy you received as a child from Santa Claus is recorded in The Archives."

Judge Stark looked at the computer for a few minutes.

Everyone waited on him, until the little girl interrupted his thoughts.

"If you still have doubts, I can show you more," she said. "I can tell you the year that each person in this room stopped believing, and what they would have received that Christmas had they continued to believe, and I can even show you some magic that is not often triggered by adults."

"What's that?" Judge Stark couldn't deny his curiosity.

"Whenever it happens that an adult non-believer becomes a believer again, which is not very often, they are moved back to the evaluation database and the event is recorded in The Archives with the symbol TB, otherwise known as a True Believer."

"So," Judge Stark said.

"Well, it so happens," she said, "that the archive record of a person in this room recently changed."

"You could have made that change yourself, while we have been talking," Judge Stark said.

"Try it, kind sir," she said. "Just type in TB beside your name on the list."

When Judge Stark did so, he saw the letters form on the page and then they disappeared. He tried again. Same result.

Having seen Judge Stark's frustration, the little girl said, "Even if I could manipulate a True Believer change in the record, which I cannot do as evidenced by your own attempts, ask yourself, kind sir, how could I do so when the flash drive was under your control in the courtroom?"

"What do you mean?" Judge Stark asked.

"The adult in this room who became a True Believer did so while court was in session today," she said. "I don't want to embarrass you, Thad, but can you confirm what I have just said."

Everyone looked to Raker, with mixed expressions of surprise and curiosity. He looked down.

"You were cross-examining Mr. Snow when it happened, is that correct?" the little girl asked.

Raker did not respond.

"How exactly did it happen?" the little girl asked. "Did you see through Mr. Snow's façade, and connect the dots that no one else could join together? Or was the timing of your change of heart simply the culmination of your efforts this past week, when you decided that you wanted to believe wholeheartedly in your client, which meant believing wholeheartedly in Santa Claus?"

Raker was not sure what to say. He had felt the change, but he couldn't explain it to himself, much less to others. When Elizabeth showed her unconditional support for him the night before, he threw himself into the task of defending Henry Edmonds, and in doing so, he felt he had stumbled on a truth, a truth that had escaped him too early in his youth.

The little girl patted Raker on the arm, and said, "It's OK, Thad, I will take it from here."

Turning to face Judge Stark, she said, "Kind sir, please look in The Archives, under the name Thad Raker, and you will see for yourself."

Judge Stark looked at Raker, and then looked at the others, not knowing whether to do what she asked, or walk right out the door, but something told him to see the thing through. He scrolled down to the Rs and found Thad Raker. It listed his gift history and the date he stopped believing in Santa Claus as a child. Out to the right of his name, Judge Stark found the initials TB, with a drop-down link for specific details. Judge Stark hit the link, and it showed the change had occurred that very morning, when Thad Raker was cross-examining Mr. Snow. And the little girl was right. The flash drive was never out of Judge Stark's sight at the time.

"Try it," the little girl said, "I know what you are thinking."

Judge Stark was miffed, but he put the curser on the letters TB, beside Raker's name, and he attempted to change them. He hit the delete key twice, causing the letters to disappear, but only briefly, because they came right back.

"Are we good?" the little girl asked.

Judge Stark didn't respond.

"OK then," she said, "It seems my work here is done and it is time for me to go, but before I do, I want to wish each of you a very Merry Christmas."

She waved politely, smiled and pointed at the laptop. Everyone looked where she pointed and when they looked back, she was gone.

1:35 p.m.

Judge Stark had returned to the bench, and the three bailiffs were standing at attention in strategic locations around the room, which was customary when the People's Court was about to hand down a ruling. Peabody, Robertson, Raker and Edmonds were all seated, waiting. The spectator pews were again filled to capacity, in anticipation of Judge Stark's decision.

"Mr. Edmonds," Judge Stark said, "please stand up to hear the Court's judgment." Raker stood up with him.

"Ms. Robertson," Judge Stark said, "please stand with Mr. Peabody. You will want to be able to hear this, too."

"It is the considered opinion of this court, Mr. Edmonds, after careful deliberation that I should find you guilty—"

Cries erupted in the courtroom, drowning out Judge Stark's words until he banged his gavel on the bench.

The room got quiet. Judge Stark said: "The next person who says a word will be held in contempt of court, and hauled off to jail, Christmas Eve or no Christmas Eve." He resettled in his chair.

"As I was saying, Mr. Edmonds, I should find you guilty as charged, but I will not. You appear to have been a bit physical with Ms. Robertson, but her memory about what happened in the tavern is now muddled and I am convinced that Mr. Snow saw nothing that night but two sets of feet, ankles and knees beneath a pool table. Thus, there is reasonable doubt as to whether you assaulted Ms. Robertson and that charge is dismissed. As for the theft of the flash drive, we had a saying in law school that possession is nine-tenths of the law, which, translated, means that the county had a better claim to the flash drive than you did when it found its way from the county's safe to your front pocket. As such, your actions could be viewed as larceny. But fortunately for you, Ms. Robertson now supports your claim to possession, so you have dodged the ball on both counts."

Judge Stark continued. "And that leaves only the question of who has the lawful right to the information on the flash drive, which has been of particular interest to the public in this case, and of great importance to Ms. Robertson, Mr. Edmonds and the mysterious Mr. Snow."

Judge Stark noticed for the first time that his wife, Kay, was sitting on one of the benches in the back of the courtroom. She smiled at him, in an encouraging way.

"It seems," Judge Stark said, "that the flash drive is rather controversial. Its ownership has been in question throughout this trial, and I must decide what happens to it.

"There has been testimony that the flash drive contains the Naughty and Nice lists and ownership of the lists is disputed. Do the lists belong to North Pole Enterprises, LLC for its business venture, or are they magical lists that belong to Santa Claus? That is the question.

"If they are only lists used by a business, then the business will lose a few profits and nothing more. But if the lists belong to Santa Claus, then the failure to release the flash drive could mean that thousands of boys and girls in this county will wake up disappointed on Christmas Day." Judge Stark paused and looked past the lawyers and the parties to the faces in the crowd. He took a deep breath, shook his head, and continued.

"Mr. Edmonds and Ms. Robertson, I have decided to release the flash drive into your joint custody, effective immediately, but on one condition and one condition only." They waited, expectantly. "You must fix the flash drive and save Christmas for the children of this county!

"God speed, and Merry Christmas."

And with that, he slammed his gavel to the bench, and shouted, "Case dismissed," at which point the audience erupted in cheers.

There was clapping, laughter and shouts of joy; a small group of attendees started to sing Christmas carols. Edmonds was hugging Raker, Robertson was hugging Peabody and school children were hugging their parents. Even the bailiffs were joining in the fun, shaking hands with the public and slapping each other on the back.

In the midst of this joyous chaos, the clerk picked up Exhibit 1 and walked it across the room to where Edmonds and Robertson were now together, enjoying the moment. She handed them the baggie and said, "I believe you two have work to do!"

Judge Stark left the People's Court for the last time in his career and walked to his chambers. Kay was sitting there waiting for him, and when he entered, she jumped up and gave him a big hug.

"That was a wonderful thing you did out there today, Augustus," she said.

"I don't know," Judge Stark said, "I think I was just smart enough to get out of the way of a moving train, or, should I say, a flying sleigh."

Meanwhile, Austin Land pecked away on his computer in the back corner of the courtroom. He was in his own little world, alone in his thoughts, as the courtroom party moved to the hallway and down to the courthouse plaza. He would have been alone in his row had it not been for someone else, whose presence he sensed before he knew for sure. When he looked up, there she was, the little girl, sitting beside him, smiling.

She leaned over against his shoulder, and looked at the article he was typing on his screen, and said, "I spell my name: S-n-o-w-f-l-a-k-e," and with that, she was gone.

5:30 p.m.

Edmonds and Robertson were still working hard when Raker walked through the door to his conference room.

"Everything going OK?" he asked, a little apprehensively, given the fact that the clock on the wall said 5:30.

It had been four hours since Raker had offered his office conference room for them to do their work, and they had not taken a break. The entire time, Robertson had been on the computer and

Edmonds had been working out the logistics of delivering the lists in the nick of time, in the event Robertson's work proved effective.

"This seems like a silly question," Raker asked, as he looked at Edmonds, "but what time does Santa Claus leave tonight?"

"He's already left," Edmonds said.

"What! After all this effort, he is already gone?"

"Don't worry," Edmonds said, "he starts in the East, six hours before the rising sun, and works his way west. If Judy can get finished in the next ten minutes, I have a rendezvous point set up that just might work."

Just then, Robertson shouted, "I got it; the security code is disabled."

"So we're done then?" Edmonds asked.

"Not quite," she said, "the program I developed needs to run in order to convert the Naughty classifications to Nice classifications, but you will be pleased to know, we are running Version 3.0."

"So, how long?" Edmonds asked.

"About ten minutes," she answered.

"That will be cutting it close," Edmonds said.

Then, after what seemed an eternity, as the clock moved to 5:40 p.m., the humming of the computer stopped and in its place was the sound of the song,

"Jingle Bell Rock." Robertson ejected the flash drive, and handed it to Edmonds, who was out the back door in an instant.

"Nice touch with the music," Raker commented.

Robertson smiled. "I just hope we finished in time," she said.

A few moments later, Edmonds was back in the conference room, with a big smile on his face, and smelling a bit like manure. Straw clung to his boots.

"Thad, my friend," he said, "I am sorry about the mess we created in the alley behind your building, but it couldn't be helped. I had to put the four-legged creature somewhere, and it was best to keep him out of sight. I must say, he certainly was ready and willing for the task, red nose and all, and now he is on a direct flight path to deliver our package to Santa. He won't fail us; I suspect they will write another song about him someday."

The mess didn't bother Raker but he did have a few final questions for Edmonds. "When the flash drive gets there, how will Santa Claus be able to use it?" he asked. "And, since the presents are already loaded in the sleigh, won't it be too late?"

Edmonds laughed, saying, "There is much we need to teach you, my friend, and much you need to leave to the imagination. To answer your first question, the sleigh is equipped with the latest technology, so when Santa Claus enters our zone, all he needs to do is plug the flash drive into the USB port in the dashboard of his sleigh, and the sleigh will steer him to the Nice homes and identify the best access points in those homes. As for your question regarding the presents, well, it's time for you to cast aside your law-school training in that adult brain of yours, and begin to think more like a child, because at this very moment, there is magic in the air."

Just then, Elizabeth Foley entered the room, and Raker introduced her to Robertson and Edmonds. He asked Edmonds for a favor. "Anything," Edmonds said, "especially after all you have done for me!"

"Well, it's like this," Raker said, reaching over and holding Elizabeth's hand, "something very important happened in my life this afternoon. The woman I love said yes to a question I should have asked a long time ago. Henry, will you be the best man in our wedding?"

After slaps on the back and hugs all around, Robertson said she needed to excuse herself, because she was meeting Peabody for dinner. "It's the second night in a row," she said.

Edmonds looked at her, and smiled, saying, in a kidding tone, "I thought I saw a little spark there."

Robertson blushed, gave Edmonds a peck on the cheek and grabbed her coat.

Raker asked his girlfriend—now fiancée—to give him just a minute. Elizabeth headed to Raker's office to gather her things and Raker turned to Edmonds.

"Henry," he said, "I want to thank you for the gift you gave me these past few days. Until you showed up in my life, I didn't have clear direction, and now I do. You changed my life, and for that, I will be forever grateful."

"It is I who should be thanking you," Edmonds replied. "Not only did you pull off the trial of the century; you gave me my freedom, facilitated the return of the Naughty and Nice lists, and you became a True Believer, which means as much as anything else."

"So what's next for you?" Raker asked.

"Ah, the future," Edmonds replied, thinking. "After Christmas, Snow and his minions will no doubt charge me for the Version 3.0 caper. I may need a good lawyer, by the way," he winked, "but for now, there is work to be done and the night is young. I must be off."

Fifteen minutes later, with snow lightly falling, Raker and Elizabeth were walking arm in arm to

Raker's car when Raker noticed a man standing alone on the street corner in a Santa suit, ringing a bell beside a Salvation Army kettle.

"Excuse me, I will be just a minute," Raker said to Elizabeth, as he left her to walk the ten steps to the corner.

When he got there, he took out his law-firm checkbook, wrote a check to the Salvation Army in the amount of twenty thousand dollars, ripped it out and deposited it in the kettle. It was the amount of his fee for the trial, which he couldn't in good conscience keep.

As Raker turned to walk away, the Santa bell ringer smiled and said, "Thank you, Thad, and Merry Christmas!"

Raker turned back and the man began to chuckle. With his last words, the Santa bell ringer tilted his head back and shouted to the world, "Merry Christmas to all, and to all a good night!"

Epilogue

Christmas morning had always come early in the Stark household, and this Christmas was no different, but as Judge Stark had aged, and as his children had moved away, Christmas morning was not the frenetic occasion it once had been, but it was no less special. He still enjoyed getting up before the sun to experience the magical feeling of the day. His tradition was to come down the steps in the peaceful, dusky dark and turn on the lights of the Christmas tree, but only those lights.

Kay Stark loved the tradition, too. On this early Christmas morning, they went down the stairs hand-in-hand, and while Judge Stark tended to lighting the tree, she fetched the newspaper off the front porch.

A moment later, she handed Judge Stark the newspaper, and said, "Augustus, here's something fun you will want to read. Merry Christmas!"

The front page article, by reporter Austin Land, was titled: "Judge Saves Christmas!" It read:

> Children today, throughout the county, are experiencing the joy and delight of Christmas morning, including the religious peace that comes with the holiday and the excitement that Santa Claus adds to the day.
>
> Yes, Lady Justice, there is a Santa's helper, or two, or three, and they work hard in every community in the world, watching over our children, and encouraging them to be Nice, not Naughty.
>
> Our community and its helper were at the precipice of a Christmas disaster this week, because of a case that unfolded in Criminal Courtroom 3150, otherwise known as the People's Court. On trial was Henry Edmonds, a homeless man to most of us, but by all accounts a true Santa's helper, one who has responsibility for the Naughty and Nice lists for this community.
>
> To make a long story short, the Naughty and Nice lists became more technical than practical, and were stored on a flash drive after the rules were changed to make it harder for children to qualify for gifts,

forcing Mr. Edmonds to search for a solution. When he did, he found himself accused of assault and larceny, and the lists became evidence in the trial against him. Because the flash drive was locked away in the evidence room at the police station until trial, Mr. Edmonds was forced to go to trial and face imprisonment on Christmas, trying to convince the Court the lists were real. It was a brave thing to do, especially when he had the ability to disappear at any time.

The director of revaluation in the county tax department, Judy Robertson, is the real heroine in this adventure, because, with the clock ticking, she was able to fix the problem, allowing all the Nice children in this county to receive gifts from Santa. Perhaps people will be kinder in the future when the tax collector comes knocking.

Local lawyers also were helpful in bringing justice to bear. Thad Raker, an excellent lawyer in our community, did a superb job exposing a particular witness as a fraud. Imagine, a witness telling the Court the Naughty and Nice lists are only corporate inventions meant to make profits.

Jason Peabody, assistant district attorney, also appears to have a bright future. Without his quick thinking, the blame might have been placed on Judy Robertson, and without her, Christmas would not have come today for thousands of children.

But there was one other person who was critical to the case, who seemed to make the biggest difference.

> At the end of the year, Judge Augustus Langhorne Stark will be retiring. He has served the justice system admirably for many years as a law-and-order judge, a fact that left everyone wondering whether Santa's helper would spend time in jail rather than time making Christmas possible. Without his good and practical judgment to release the flash drive to the person who could fix it, and to the person who could deliver it in time to Santa Claus, Christmas would have been doomed. The outcome was as special as a Snowflake.
>
> So rest easy, members of our peaceful community, and know this: Your tax dollars do work, especially when they help to keep the Halls of Justice open, and the spirit of Christmas alive.

Judge Stark put down the newspaper, and looked at the Christmas tree, thinking how beautiful it looked, as he reflected on the trial.

He did what he did, he thought, not because he was a True Believer, as the little girl had called Raker, but because it seemed to be the most practical thing to do under the circumstances.

He knew he was playing into the Santa frenzy with his decision, but in the end, he had decided not to spoil Christmas for the believers. He was comfortable with what he had done, even though it was not, technically, by the book.

As he was admiring the Christmas ornaments, he noticed a wrapped package leaning up against the tree.

"Dear," he called out, "I thought we agreed there would be no gifts this year, except for the cost of our trip to visit the grandchildren."

"What are you talking about?" she asked.

He got up, walked to the tree and picked up the package.

"This," he said, holding the package up in his hand for her to see.

"I have no idea where that came from," she said, and by the surprised look on her face, he believed her.

He looked more closely at the package. It was long and narrow and had a card on it shaped like a snowflake, with a note, saying, "Merry Christmas, kind sir," in very pretty handwriting.

After a minute passed, with Judge Stark looking at the package, his wife said, "Are you going to open it, or just stare it into submission like one of those lawyers in your courtroom?"

Fine, he thought to himself, and tore the paper from the box. Seeing what he held, he sat down on the floor by the Christmas tree, with his legs crossed, much like he had done when he was the excited seven-year-old boy who still believed.

Sitting on his lap was a vintage Red Ryder BB gun with a compass in the stock.

They don't make these anymore, he thought, at least not this style, because he had seen what they were selling these days, and they were not the same. This was an authentic, mint-condition, 1950s-style Red Ryder BB gun with a compass in the stock.

And then Judge Stark started to laugh, and he laughed like he hadn't laughed in years.

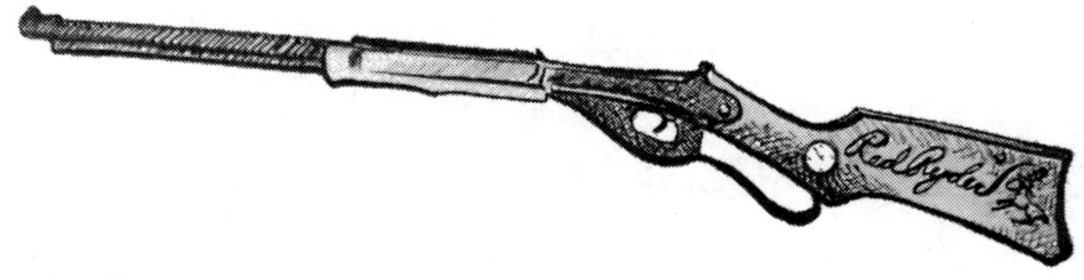

The End

Acknowledgements

The original version of this story was written in 2014 between Thanksgiving and Christmas. When it seemed possible one night that I might be able to finish the story by Christmas Day, I decided I would make it a Christmas gift for my family. Suddenly, I had a deadline. And with that, and just like the characters in this story, I was constantly appearing and disappearing as the deadline grew closer and feeling and acting upon the stress of an approaching Christmas Day. Finally, at around 11:45 p.m. on Christmas Eve, I pushed away from my keyboard and began to print the copies I would share the next morning. My thanks (and apologies) go to my wife, Janet, daughter Jordan and son Hamlin, who put up with my obsession "to finish" in those last few days before Christmas.

I also am grateful to my larger family, friends and colleagues who took the time to read the first version of this story. Your constructive feedback and encouragement led me to clean it up for a larger audience. You know who you are.

My appreciation also goes to Nora Gaskin Esthimer (Chapel Hill, North Carolina), my editor, and Lystra Books & Literary Services, my publisher, for turning my story into a book. They pulled together a great team, provided excellent feedback and kept the book completion train running on time.

Truth be told, the editing process made me feel like we were pruning a forest with a handsaw, reminding me of the old saying that "if I had had more time, I would have written you a shorter letter." My very sharp-penciled copyeditor, Karen Van Neste Owen (Richmond, Virginia), pressed me to say more with less, something many lawyers have a hard time doing, and she educated me on things like punctuation and capitalization. She and Nora also pushed me to clarify the text and fill in the missing pieces. Their editorial work inspired me to bring fresh material to the story, while "helping" me to consign more than three thousand original words to the recycle bin. Though my gratitude is warranted, this sort of feels like thanking my athletic coaches for that special summer workout program they designed.

While the words of the story continued to be "under construction," I was able to enjoy the pleasant diversion of illustrations showing up from time to time in my mailbox. I was hoping for creative covers for the book, and fun sketches for the interior, and Susanne Discenza Frueh (Norman,

Oklahoma) delivered perfectly. Thanks, Sue, for making me smile when I look at your drawings. I want to visit the Tipsy Tavern you have depicted and have that one drink.

Thanks also to Beth Tashery Shannon the Frogtown Bookmaker (Georgetown, Kentucky), for creating the design of the book. You made the colors pop, the margins work, the tweets tweet and the words easy on these aging eyes. I had no idea that designing a book would involve so many moving parts, but you made the parts move in concert.

I also am grateful to those readers whose comments appear in this book and on the back cover. I appreciate your time and I am humbled by your characterizations of the story.

Thanks also to Julia Barnard, for your editorial help, and to my assistant, Angela Bias, for your help and input.

And to my wife Janet, thank you for your feedback on the story and your encouragement to "finish what I started," which, I know, is a Wade family rule, but a rule I have been known to violate when it comes to writing fiction on the side. You're the best!

Finally, I thank you, the reader, for spending some of your precious time in Courtroom 3150. I hope you enjoyed your visit.

Landis Wade is a civil trial lawyer, arbitrator and mediator in Charlotte, N.C. He is a 1979 graduate of Davidson College, where he majored in history and played varsity football, and a 1983 graduate of Wake Forest Law School, where he was a member of the Law Review and the National Moot Court team. Landis is married, has two adult children and two rescue dogs. He enjoys sports, traveling with his family, and spending time at their cabin in Watauga County, N.C., where he likes to fly-fish, hike, bike, read and write.

Contact the author: thechristmasheist@gmail.com
Like us on Facebook:
www.facebook.com/thechristmasheist

CPSIA information can be obtained at www.ICGtesting.com
Printed in the USA
LVOW06s1138161115

462751LV00003B/8/P